HOW

DO YOU...
HUG AN
ANGEL?

A DEVOTIONAL NOVEL
FOR JUNIOR HIGHERS

Other Herbie books by Mary Lou Carney:

Angel in My Attic
Angel in My Backpack
Angel in My Locker
Wrestling with an Angel

HOW DO YOU... HUG AN ANGEL?

A DEVOTIONAL NOVEL FOR JUNIOR HIGHERS

MARY LOU CARNEY

ZondervanPublishingHouse
Grand Rapids, Michigan

A Division of HarperCollinsPublishers

How Do You Hug an Angel?
Copyright © 1993 by Mary Lou Carney
All rights reserved

Requests for information should be directed to:
Zondervan Publishing House
Grand Rapids, Michigan 49530

Library of Congress Cataloging-in-Publication Data

Carney, Mary Lou, 1949–
   How do you hug an angel? : a devotional novel for junior highers /
Mary Lou Carney.
      p. cm.
   Summary: A collection of daily devotions tells the story of a
guardian angel named Herbie who helps a young girl deal with the
death of her mother, regaining her hearing, and going to middle
school.
   ISBN 0-310-59411-1 (pbk.)
   1. Junior high school students—Prayer-books and devotions—
English. 2. Devotional calendars. 3. Christian life—1960—
Juvenile literature. [1. Prayer books and devotions. 2.
Christian life.] I. Title.
BV4850.C355 1993
242'.63—dc20   93-22207
                                                                 CIP
                                                                  AC

All Scripture quotations, unless otherwise noted, are taken from the *Holy
Bible: New International Version* (North American Edition). Copyright © 1973,
1978, 1984, by the International Bible Society. Used by permission of
Zondervan Bible Publishers.

Edited by Dave Lambert and Lori J. Walburg
Cover design by Larry Taylor
Illustrations by Matt Mew

Printed in the United States of America

93 94 95 96 97 / DH / 5 4 3 2 1

*For all
the huggers
in my life*

This is a book of devotions ...

It may not *look* like a devotional book, and it certainly doesn't *read* like one.

But it is.

We wanted to give you a different kind of devotional book. A real action-packed novel. We thought you'd have more fun with it. And we thought you'd be interested in Elise, too—a middle-school girl a lot like you with the same problems you have, from worrying about fitting in at her new school to looking forward to her first date. Then there's the fact that her mom died and now her dad is dating their next-door neighbor.

You don't have a Herbie the angel in your life—at least not that you can see and talk to. We just made him up.

But we hope Herbie and Elise—two made-up characters—will help you to think about a God who is real. And about how that God can make a difference in the everyday, middle-school problems *you* face.

Chapter 1.

"Try harder!" Elise urged, jabbing her shovel into the grass.

"You'd need 'Mr. Universe' to dig through this stuff," Garren said. "How can dirt be so hard?"

"I think it's the cement they used when they set this thing." Elise banged the face of the sign with her shovel. A loud *brong-ong-ong* echoed down the empty street. Elise covered her ears. "Ow! What an ugly sound."

Garren laughed. "Wait until you hear Ears burp after a giant cola at McDonald's. It registers on the Richter Scale!"

Elise sighed and leaned against the sign. DEAF CHILD IN AREA. Why hadn't the city come to take it down? Her dad had called the street department, even gone to a town council meeting. This sign was part of her past—and Elise wanted it gone.

"Forget it for now," Garren said, shouldering his shovel. "We've only got a week before school starts. Let's go for a bike ride or shoot a few baskets or do *something* fun!"

A week. Elise's stomach lurched at the thought. Hinkle Creek Middle School. She'd grilled Garren all summer. What was it like? Were the teachers mean? Would the other kids like her? What should she wear? It was all too much, too fast. First the operation, and now a whole new world. A whole new, *noisy* world.

Elise stood staring into her closet. She needed clothes, but what kind? Last year, at the hearing impaired school, they'd all worn uniforms. Dark blue jumpers and crisp white blouses. Predictable. Safe. But Hinkle Creek would be different. The cool kids would have cool clothes. But the rest of the kids . . .

"Mind if I come in?"

Elise turned to see her father standing just outside her door. "Of course not. Just taking inventory."

"Inventory?"

"School's starting, Daddy. I need some school clothes."

"Oh, of course. I should have thought of that. Your mother, she was always the one . . ."

Elise turned back to her closet. Mother. She would know just what to buy. When she closed her eyes tightly, Elise could still see her mother's face. Smell her sweet perfume. Feel the softness of the silk shirts she always wore. If only mother were here.

". . . a trip to the mall. Surely a sales clerk could help . . ."

Elise realized her father was talking to her. She turned to him and smiled. He fumbled with his hat, running his thumb around the brim the way he did when he was flustered. "Sure, the mall. I'm bound to find just the right things," she said. *What does Daddy know about buying school clothes? He's worn those same suits as long as I can remember. I guess when you're a philosophy professor, you're so caught up in big thoughts that you don't have time to think about the latest styles.* "We'll get a frozen yogurt afterwards." Elise forced herself to sound cheerful. "It'll be just like old times."

But even after all the practice—two years and one month of practice—Elise still had trouble pretending that anything was the same since her mother's death.

The hallway was wide and long. Swirling blue smoke snaked up the walls. At the far end a shadowy figure was motioning her forward. "I'm coming!" Elise called. But her feet felt like lead, and her movements were awkward, like a slow motion replay from an old movie. The figure moved away from her. Elise felt her chest tighten. "Wait! I'm coming!" She willed herself to move faster. Faster. Pounding filled her ears and then a roaring like a thousand freight trains. For a brief second, the figure turned toward her, but shadows cloaked its face. Then suddenly it was loping through the blackness, going further and further away. "Don't leave me!" Elise screamed as smoke swirled around her, clutching at her lungs, plunging her into darkness.

Elise awoke sitting up in her bed, her hair soaked with perspiration. Her breath came in gasps. The dream. It had been months since she'd had it. Elise pulled the covers around her, realizing that even though she was sweating she was cold. It was always the same. Running. Aching. The longing to reach . . . to reach what? Sometimes she almost made it to the end of the hallway. Almost, but not quite.

She pushed back the covers and plodded toward the

bathroom for a drink of water. "It's your stress dream," her father had said matter-of-factly the day Elise told him about it. "Many people have a recurring dream when they feel pressured by circumstances or a new situation."

Everything's so logical to Daddy, Elise thought, sipping the water and staring at herself in the mirror. Her mother's eyes stared back. Quickly, Elise turned on the light. Her face looked white—too white. *If only I'd gotten a suntan this summer. I'm sure all the cool kids will have suntans.* She flipped off the light and headed back toward her bedroom.

> *Be strong and courageous. Do not be terrified; do not be discouraged, for the Lord your God will be with you wherever you go.*
> *(Joshua 1:9)*

Chapter 2

And that's when she saw it. A light, soft and shimmery, shining from the foot of her bed. *Am I dreaming?* she wondered. She rubbed her eyes and looked again. Darkness. Carefully Elise got into bed, running her hand under the sheets before she crawled between them. She closed her eyes and willed the bad dream away. *Flicker, flicker.* Elise opened her eyes. *What was that? A firefly?* She raised up on one elbow and looked around her room. Nothing unusual . . . but, wait. *Did I leave my closet light on?* Cautiously, Elise made her way to the closet. She put her ear to the door and listened. A humming sound came from inside. *Grasshoppers?* Reaching for the fly swatter on her dresser, she threw open the closet door.

She'd never seen anything like it before. *An alien?* He was dressed all in white with huge, silvery wings fluttering on his back. He wore high-top sneakers and—was it possible?—a halo! Elise stood frozen in place. *I've got to get Daddy.*

The creature turned toward her. "Ooph! You've taken me quite by surprise, I'm afraid. I know the

contents of this storage area are important to you, and I was trying to figure out why." He put away the tiny spiral he was writing on and turned toward Elise. She gripped the fly swatter tighter. A sound like rippling wind chimes filled the room. "Do put that thing down. I'm hardly an insect to be squashed by a ventilated piece of plastic."

"What . . . what are you?"

The creature flew past her in a flurry of sparkling dust and flutter. He landed on her window sill, brushed the wrinkles out of his robe, straightened his halo, and smiled. All his teeth were gold! "Isn't it obvious?"

Elise shook her head, moving a little closer.

The creature seemed annoyed. "Think hard, Elise. Haven't you ever seen anything like me before?"

He knows my name. "Um . . . you look sort of like Tinkerbell."

"Hardly!"

And then Elise realized she *had* seen something that looked a lot like the creature. But that was silly. He couldn't be . . . "You sort of look like an . . . an angel."

"Applause, applause, kid!" The creature took off his halo and bowed from the waist. "Herbekiah's the name, but you can call me Herbie."

I'm still asleep, Elise thought. *Talk about a weird dream! Wait till I tell Daddy about this one.*

"I'm not a dream, and telling your father about me isn't a very good idea."

"How did you know what I was thinking?" Elise gasped.

Herbie yawned. "No big trick for an angel, kid. Now, let's get down to business." He hovered, cross-legged, in front of the window and pulled his spiral from his sleeve. A tiny gold pencil magically appeared.

Cautiously, Elise sat down on the edge of the bed, still clutching the fly swatter.

"I've been sent here . . ."

"Sent? From where?"

Herbie sighed and pointed out the window. Stars splashed across the late summer sky. "There, of course."

"Space?"

"Heaven!" Herbie shook his head. "Humans," he mumbled. Then he said briskly, "I'm to be your guardian angel this year while you attend"—he turned back to his spiral—"Hinkle Creek Middle School."

"Guardian angel?"

"That's right."

"Just mine?"

"I don't do groups," Herbie said, flying over and perching on Elise's pillow. "Just you. And judging from my pre-flight notes, you're going to need my full-time attention."

"Am I in danger?"

Herbie laughed, and the sound of wind chimes again filled the room. "No, not in the traditional sense of the word. But there are those cheerleaders and Mr. Hoffer and that contest." Herbie slipped the spiral back in his sleeve. "Look, kid, I'm here to help you. New school, new sounds." Herbie touched his ear. Then he signed, "Can be rough."

Elise dropped the fly swatter and wrapped her arms around her knees. "You know about the deafness?"

"And the operation. The world of sound takes some getting used to."

14

"Don't I know it! I wish the world had a volume control so I could turn everything down!" she said. *I'm talking to a figment of my imagination. Weird. Maybe I'm going nuts or something.*

Suddenly Elise's pillow flew through the air and landed with a thud against her back. "Hey!"

"Can a figment of your imagination do that?" Herbie asked, his gold teeth glinting in the moonlight.

"I . . . I don't know. All I know is I want to go back to sleep. And not dream," she added softly.

"Done!" Herbie said.

Elise looked around her. She was snuggled into her bed and the room was dark. Totally dark, except for the moonlight splashing onto the foot of her blanket. *Did I dream that whole conversation with some alien . . . angel? Too weird!* she thought, noticing the flicker of light in her closet just before she drifted off to dreamless sleep.

☆　☆　☆

See, I am sending an angel ahead of you to guard you along the way and to bring you to the place I have prepared. Pay attention to him and listen to what he says.
(Exodus 23:20–21)

Chapter 3.

Elise had never seen anything like it. From one end of the hall to the other, kids swarmed out of doors and into the hallway. Yells of "Wait up!" and "What class do you have next?" mingled with the banging of lockers and the sounds of hundreds of sneakers padding against the tile floor. Clutching her books to her chest, Elise tried to move into the swirling throng. She felt herself being pushed along and checked the room numbers of the doors she was passing. 205, 203. Where was room 178? There. At last!

She slipped into the door and took the first seat. Social studies—Mr. Hoffer. Garren had warned her about him. "He likes to be the boss," Garren had said. "So make sure you have everything you need—pencils and paper and junk like that." Elise checked her notebook. Everything seemed in order. For the thousandth time she stroked her bright folders and new pencils, smushed her thumb into the fat pink eraser. School supplies. She'd forgotten how much she enjoyed getting all these new things every fall. Homeschooling with her mother had been fun, but . . .

16

Suddenly Elise felt a nudge on her arm. Ears.

"Hey," he said, clicking off his tape player and pulling out his earphones. "See you got 'The Beast,' too." He cocked his head toward Mr. Hoffer, who had just walked in and set a cup of coffee on his desk.

Elise smiled and nodded. What was Ears doing here in seventh-grade social studies? Hadn't he and Garren been in the same grade last year?

But before she could ask, the bell clanged the beginning of class. Elise cringed and stared at the vibrating metal box on the wall. Long after it stopped ringing, the sound seemed to echo deep inside her.

Why is everything so noisy? Elise thought, standing just inside the cafeteria and holding her tray as though it might jump out of her hands at any moment. The room seemed to shimmer with a massive whir, like sounds of giant insects. And movement. Everywhere kids seemed to be tossing food into the trash, throwing silverware into bins, jostling each other in good-natured fun. *I can't do it*, Elise thought, feeling her chest tighten and sweat start to form on her palms. She wanted to drop her tray, to cover her ears. Lunchtime at the hearing impaired school had been so orderly. And quiet. Gentle hands fluttering as the girls talked to one another in sign language. Sweet, silent laughter. And where was she supposed to sit? Was there some kind of law that said cool kids sat together? Impulsively, Elise tossed her food into a trash can, plopped her tray on a moving black conveyor belt, and headed outside.

Better, she thought, feeling the rays of late summer sun on her face as she walked to the back of the building, away from the game of touch football just beginning on the grassy playing field. She sat down under a huge maple tree, leaning her back against its trunk.

"Here, kid. Skipping lunch is no way to start off your school year."

Elise looked up to see . . . that *creature* from the other night. He was holding out a perfect, shiny apple.

"Go ahead," he laughed, as the sound of wind chimes echoed on the breeze. "I'm your guardian angel, not the witch from *Snow White!*"

She reached for the apple, wondering if it would really be there. *Can a figment of my imagination carry fruit?*

The apple was real. Suddenly Elise realized she was hungry. She bit into the crisp fruit, never taking her eyes off . . . *it.*

"So far, so good, wouldn't you say?" He fluttered down and stood on the grass near Elise. "I mean, you've managed to find all your classes, even if you were late twice. And tomorrow the cafeteria will seem a little more tame, once you know a few faces and can prepare yourself to handle the noise."

Can I really have a guardian angel? Elise felt the apple juice dribble down her chin.

Herbie sighed. "Why is it so hard for you to believe in me, kid?"

Elise wiped her chin with the back of her hand. "I don't know. I guess because I never . . . well, never saw an angel before."

Herbie flew up and paced in midair, waving his arms like a politician. "You believe in lots of other things you've never seen before! Jupiter and electricity and

18

ocean currents. And what about heaven. You believe in that, don't you?"

Instantly, Elise pictured her mother. In heaven. Of course she believed in heaven! If her mom wasn't in heaven, then she was in that dark hole. That worm-filled, clammy hole. Elise nodded. "I believe in heaven."

"Well, then," Herbie said, landing again. "Believe in me. That's where I come from."

Elise chewed the last bit of apple slowly. A guardian angel. Her very own. That would be a pretty sweet deal, a real advantage in this strange, noisy place. Could he help her with her homework? Show her where to sit in the cafeteria? Let her locker open every time she spinned the combo? Make her popular?

Might as well believe, she thought as she walked to a nearby trash barrel. *My life's due for a few fairy tale happily-ever-afters.*

Herbie flew after her.

"Can anyone else see or hear you?" she asked.

"Nope."

"Good. Now," Elise said as she dug into her notebook for her schedule. "Let's lay in a flight pattern for room 122. Music."

"Roger Wilco," Herbie said, saluting. And leaving a trail of angel dust, he headed for the double doors on the side of the building.

Call to me and I will answer you and tell you great and unsearchable things you do not know.
(Jeremiah 33:3)

Chapter 4

"I'll never get used to middle school," Elise said, shifting her book bag to her shoulder as she walked.

Garren laughed. "Sure you will! It's only been two weeks."

"Feels more like two years."

"You just need to get to know a few people. Get involved in something."

"Like what, wrestling?"

"Nah," Garren said, smiling, "we've already got our 103-pounder. How about cheerleading?"

Elise frowned. "No way. I can't even imagine all the noise a crowd in a gymnasium must make!" She slowed down and placed her hand on Garren's arm. "I can't tell you how loud everything seems. After all those years of fading sounds and then silence. Now, BOOM! When the doctor did that surgery last summer, he never told me it would be like this. He never warned me . . ."

Garren stopped and faced her. "And if he had? What would you have done?"

Slowly, Elise smiled. "I would have said, 'Make me hear, Doc. I've got to know if Garren's voice sounds like Clint Eastwood or Kermit the Frog!'"

Garren laughed, and in his very lowest voice said, "Well, I guess I made your day!"

The first bell rang just as they reached the edge of the school yard.

"Got to run!" Garren said, jogging across the parking lot toward the gym. "Coach wants to see us in the wrestling room before first period." He looked back over his shoulder at Elise, "Remember what I said. Get to know somebody!"

English class. Elise's favorite. "Today we'll divide up into pairs for our poetry projects." Miss Rosetti smiled, and Elise thought she looked just like one of those models on the cover of the magazines at the grocery store checkout stand.

"Okay, kid. This is your big chance!" Herbie stood on the edge of Elise's desk, a tiny gold spiral in his hand. "According to my records, you're pretty good at this poetry stuff."

Elise smiled. It almost seemed normal now, having a guardian angel appear at any moment. *Suppose anybody else at Hinkle Creek has ever had a guardian angel?* she wondered. Maybe sometime she'd ask Herbie.

". . . can choose who you want to work with. But remember, this project is worth three letter grades, so choose carefully!" Miss Rosetti turned to the board and began writing what each group would be expected to do.

The room buzzed with kids signaling their friends, making sure they would be with someone they knew, somebody they liked. Of course Alissa would be with Dawn. Elise couldn't ever remember seeing one without the other—especially on the days they wore their cheerleading uniforms.

Miss Rosetti turned to face them. "Ready? Find your partners!"

Desks scraped across the floor as everyone scurried to be near their choice of partners. Elise didn't look up. She could feel the excitement, hear the giggles of the girls, the "All right's!" of the boys. *Maybe the floor will open up. Any minute. And I won't have to be here by myself.* Elise sensed someone was standing beside her.

"Hi."

Looking up, Elise recognized the girl from the far corner of the room. What was her name?

"Guess you need a partner, huh?"

Elise nodded. "You too?"

"Yep." The girl pushed her glasses up on her nose and reached for a nearby desk. "Actually, you're in luck. I'm smarter than a six-pack of those cheerleaders. And I haven't giggled since I learned to walk."

Elise laughed. "I'm Elise."

"I know. You're new. My name's Riley. Riley Blohm."

"Riley?"

Riley waved the question aside with her hand. "Don't question, just accept. That's what I had to do."

"Well, I guess we're a team then," Elise said. "Nice to meet you, Riley."

"Ditto. Now, let's get all the details of this piddly project so we can can the competition." Riley took a chewed-up pencil out of her pocket and began copying

22

the information off the board. "After all, what's a metaphor for if not to raise your grade some more?"

"Yeah, right," Elise said, watching Dawn and Alissa as they bent close together over a shared spiral.

A man that hath friends must show himself friendly.

(Proverbs 18:24 KJV)

Chapter 5

It was raining. Hard. Blue-gray sheets slanted into the ground, pounding the pavement into puddles. Cars with wipers swiping and engines running were lined up all along the curb. Mothers, mostly. Come to rescue their kids from the unexpected shower. Elise pulled up the hood of her jacket and pushed open the door. *Well, my mom won't be coming to rescue me. Not now. Or tomorrow. Or ever.* Elise imagined the rain on her mother's grave. Did the sound echo underground? Did the pitty-pats land on the cold, gray vault that held her mother?

"Elise! Elise!"

Elise looked through raindrop-rimmed eyelashes at the car that had stopped alongside her. A woman was leaning toward the open window. "Can I give you a ride home?"

It was Garren's mom. "Sure!" Elise ran toward the door Mrs. Gillum had thrown open.

"What a downpour!" Mrs. Gillum said, pulling back into the line of traffic.

"That's for sure."

"I came to pick up Garren, but that Coach Cannon wanted him to stay after and start body conditioning. I'll never get used to his wrestling. It makes me so nervous to think about another boy trying to hurt him . . ." Her voice trailed off. Elise tried to think of something to say, but without luck.

So they rode in silence, Mrs. Gillum paying attention to the slippery roads and kids hurrying to get home. Elise could hear rain dripping off her jacket and onto the vinyl seat. It was an awkward silence, not the kind Elise and her father shared when he was reading the latest issue of *Harpers* and she was doing word searches. Thinking back, Elise couldn't remember a time when she had ever before been alone with Mrs. Gillum, even though she and Garren did live next door. Elise looked out of the corner of her eye toward her. She looked different, somehow. Maybe it was her hair. Or that bright lipstick she was wearing. How long had it been since Garren's dad had moved to Boston? Six months? Anyway, Mrs. Gillum seemed to be holding up pretty well for a divorced lady.

"Here we are." She paused in front of Elise's house before turning into her own driveway.

Elise gathered her things. "Thanks a lot."

"No problem, dear."

Elise slammed the car door shut and ran through the rain to her own front porch. Once in its shelter, she threw off her hood and stood listening to the rain. *Listening.* It was a magic word for Elise. Something she had longed to do for years. And now she heard it all. The hard splatter of rain against the sidewalk, a sound remarkably like frying bacon. The gurgle of water rushing through the nearby gutter pipe. The peppering pounding on the porch roof.

"Pretty inspiring, huh, kid?" Herbie stood on the railing, holding a gold umbrella.

"One of my favorite things—rainstorms. When my hearing began to worsen, I used to press my ear to the window and try to hear the drops on the pane." A clap of thunder made Elise jump. "Boy, this is really a big one!"

Herbie flew into the porch, shaking the rain off his umbrella and slipping it magically up his sleeve. "You think *this* is rain, you should have been on the ark!"

"What ark?"

"*The* ark!" Herbie humphed.

Elise pulled a key from her pocket and unlocked the front door. "As in *Noah's* ark?"

"The very same!"

"You were on Noah's ark?"

"Uh huh."

"Wow!" Elise said, hanging her jacket over a kitchen chair to dry. "You must be about a zillion years old!"

"I'm ageless, kid. All us angels are."

The phone began ringing. It echoed through the empty house and made Elise wish for the thousandth time that her dad could arrange his schedule at the university so he could be home when she got home.

"Hello?" The receiver still felt a bit awkward to Elise, and she still experienced a thrill when she could hear, clearly, the voice on the other end.

"It's me. Riley."

"Oh, hello, Riley."

Silence seemed to crackle on the line.

"How are you?" Elise said. *Stupid question!*

A low laugh came back. "Wet, like all the other poor louts who walked home in this downpour. I wanted to know if you want to go to the main library tomorrow after school—assuming, of course, that all the thoroughfares in town haven't been reduced to canals by then."

"The main library?"

"Yeah, the one downtown. Haven't you ever been?"

"Well, no . . . not exactly." Elise was embarrassed to think about all the places she'd never been. Would Riley think she was a baby if she knew?

"Time you did, then. We'll take the bus. Bring some money for the fare. And a few extra quarters in case we need to copy anything on the Xerox machine."

Click.

Elise pulled the phone with its loud dial tone away from her ear. "Good-bye to you, too," she said into thin air. What a strange girl this Riley was. Still, she had asked Elise to be her partner. And she had called her. Maybe this could turn into something besides just an English-partner relationship.

Maybe.

Praise be to God . . . who comforts us in all our troubles, so that we can comfort those in any trouble with the comfort we ourselves have received from God.

(*2 Corinthians 1:3–4*)

28

Chapter 6

"Quiet down, class!" Miss Rosetti seemed all business today. She turned to the stack of papers on her desk. "I have finished grading your projects, and I must say some of you are going to be disappointed in your grade. You were supposed to read widely, lots of different poets and styles before choosing your sample works. And many of your 'poet profiles' read surprisingly like encyclopedia copy."

Several of the boys in the back snickered. Elise was glad she and Riley had spent time at the main library. Had taken time to put their information in their own words. And Riley's computer had made the whole thing look like a college paper. Still, it made Elise's stomach lurch to see Miss Rosetti like this. *What if she hates our project?* Elise worried. *Will Riley blame me?*

And then Miss Rosetti was calling names. One person from each group went forward and claimed their project. Several kids groaned when they saw their grades. Alissa gasped out loud and made a face at Dawn before she slammed the papers facedown on her desk.

Then it was over—except Elise and Riley hadn't gotten their project back. Where was it? Why hadn't she called their names?

Elise looked toward Riley, but she was reading a library book and didn't seem to care what was happening.

"And now," Miss Rosetti said, smiling for the first time. "I've saved the best for last. Here's a fine example of a project that was taken seriously by its participants. Elise and Riley."

The room seemed suddenly silent. Elise looked toward Riley, but she was still reading. Or at least pretending to read. So Elise walked to the front of the room, her heart booming as she felt everyone's eyes on her.

"Fine work," Miss Rosetti said.

"Thanks," Elise mumbled.

She couldn't help but notice the scowl on Dawn's face when she passed her. And when the bell sounded the end of class, several boys made kissing sounds as they passed her. *Why are they doing that?* Elise wondered. Were they being fresh?

"Ignore them," Riley said, glancing at the report grade before taking Elise's elbow and steering her out of the room. "Their IQ and shoe size are the same. Maybe the shoe size is bigger," she called back over her shoulder as she disappeared into the crowd.

But Elise had no doubt what Alissa meant when she bumped into her and said, "Teacher's pet." Then she and Dawn hurried down the hall, whispering and looking back at Elise—and laughing.

Elise pushed her way into the hallway crowd. All around her kids were laughing and talking. She saw two girls exchange notes as they passed. Lowering her head, Elise tried to hurry to her next class.

"Good grade, kid!"

Elise looked up to see Herbie fluttering over her. "I guess so."

"Guess so?" Herbie landed on her shoulder. "According to my research, this *A* mark is the best possible."

"Yeah, it is. But maybe I shouldn't have done such a fancy report. Riley was so gung-ho to get the highest grade."

"Listen, kid," Herbie said, leaning close to her ear so Elise could catch every word. "Doing your best is always the best course of action."

"Always?" Elise asked as she paused in front of the door to her health class.

Herbie nodded. "Absolutely." He pointed his finger skyward. "He gives every human being talents and abilities. But it's up to each one of you to make the most of what you have."

"I just hope my 'making the most' doesn't cost me a chance to be friends with the popular girls," Elise said as she stepped into the classroom.

"You can take it home first, if you want to," Elise said. "Show your parents."

Riley banged her locker door shut. Elise winced at the sound. "My folks have seen enough *A*'s to last them till the year 2050. Besides, my dad's got his nose in a big computer project and won't be interested in much else for a few days."

"What about . . . your mother?" Elise asked, knowing how proud her own mother would have been of the good grade.

"My mother," Riley said, a cold sound coming into her voice, "is out of town on business. Again. Or is it *still*."

Elise stood beside her, the report in her hand, unsure what any of that meant. Sometimes Riley talked in riddles. And it could be pretty annoying, especially if they were going to be friends.

"Look," Riley said, a softer tone replacing the coldness. "You take it for the rest of the week. Wow the old folks at home. I'll take it next week."

"Okay," Elise said, gently placing the project into her folder. "But it's just my dad. My mom's . . . my mom's dead." *Dead*. The word had a bad taste to it.

Riley looked surprised. "I didn't know. I'm sorry. Really."

"It's okay," Elise said as they walked outside.

But it wasn't okay, and Elise wondered if it ever could be.

> God has given each of us the ability to do certain
> things well.
> (Romans 12:6 TLB)

Chapter 7

"Why do they hate me?" Elise pulled the holder off her ponytail and began brushing her long, ash-blond hair.

"Who?" Herbie asked, studying his gold teeth in the mirror.

Elise stopped brushing her hair and looked at him. "I thought you knew everything."

"Only the Boss knows everything," Herbie said, nodding heavenward. "But I do know who you're talking about. Alissa and Dawn, right?"

Elise flinched as the brush caught on a tangle. "Uh huh. I've been trying to get up the nerve to talk to them ever since school started. They're just so . . . so *with it*. They know everybody. And get invited to all the parties. Their clothes are always perfect, and they never *ever* look stupid or say dumb things."

"This must be what you humans refer to as the 'in' group?"

Elise sighed. "I guess so. But I don't think there's much chance of my ever being let in." She tossed the brush onto the dresser. "Especially after the big deal Miss Rosetti made about my report."

"*Your* report?"

"Well, mine and Riley's. And that's another thing. Riley. Sometimes she acts like she wants to be friends, and sometimes she acts like she's somewhere off in space and I'm an unwelcome alien."

"As I recall from my past assignments, you humans are a moody lot."

Elise pulled back her covers and crawled into bed. "Sometimes I'm not sure I even want to be friends with Riley."

"Why's that?" Herbie asked, fluttering to a soft landing on Elise's pillow.

"Well, she's definitely not part of the 'in' group. I don't think she'd want to be even if they asked her. And if I'm friends with her . . . well, they may think I feel the same way about things that she does."

"Let me get this straight. You don't want to be friends with your only friend because you think these two girls who aren't your friends won't be your friends if you do?" Herbie scratched his head through his halo.

Elise clicked off the light beside her bed. "Oh, Herbie. You just don't understand."

"Do you think friendship is something that somebody just invented? Hardly!" Herbie huffed. "It's been around as long as humankind itself. The Bible is full of people who were great friends! Joshua and Caleb, David and Jonathan, Paul and Barnabas, Jonah and the whale."

"Jonah and the whale?"

"Okay, maybe not Jonah and the whale," Herbie said. "The point is, few things are as important as the friends a human chooses."

Elise raised herself up on one elbow and looked at Herbie. "What do you mean by that?"

"Because you people are a lot like chameleons."

"You mean those slimy little lizards?"

Herbie chuckled. "Actually, chameleons aren't too fond of your species either. You see, chameleons can change their color to blend in with their surroundings."

"So?" Elise said, yawning. "I'm not planning to turn green or anything."

"No, but people become more like the people they spend their time with. Spend your time with a grouch, and what happens?"

Elise shrugged. "I guess you could get grouchy, too."

"Precisely," Herbie said, stamping the pillow for emphasis. "All kinds of character traits—from selfishness to kindness—are contagious."

"Well, there's nothing wrong with being popular! And the way to be popular is to have popular friends. That's one thing I've learned in middle school already." Elise plopped down on her pillow and pulled the covers up to her chin.

"But school's not out yet, kid," Herbie said. "And you still have a few other things to learn. Right?"

Elise squeezed her eyes shut and pretended not to hear.

Bad company corrupts good character.
(1 Corinthians 15:33)

Chapter

Elise stood on tiptoe, looking for Garren's "Chicago Bulls" cap. Kids streamed out the door, hurrying to their buses or down the crowded sidewalks toward home. *Where is he?* Elise wondered. The last thing Garren had said that morning was to meet him after school, and they'd walk home together.

"Yo! Hello!" Ears whirred to a stop near Elise, his in-line skates moving back and forth to some rhythm that pulsed through headphones plugged into his cassette player. "Looking for the big guy?"

Elise nodded. "Garren said he'd meet me here."

"No can do," Ears said, clicking off his tape player. "The man has planted himself in the library to do some research for world geography."

"Oh," Elise said. "Well, thanks for telling me."

"No problem—and neither is walking a ways your way. Okay?"

Elise shifted her books in her arms. "Uh . . . sure."

They walked in silence, Ears gliding along on his skates beside Elise. "So, how do you like Hinkle Creek?" he asked.

Elise shrugged. "Okay, I guess. A little noisier than I'd expected." She smiled shyly, remembering the time last year when Ears had almost hit her with his skateboard because she hadn't heard him coming.

"You'll get used to it."

"That's what they say."

The smile Ears usually wore faded. "Wish I had a

few new things to get used to. This year is like a black-and-white rerun of last year."

Elise knew Ears was repeating seventh grade. Garren had told her that Ears's scores on the standardized tests they took at the end of last year hadn't been high enough. She glanced toward Ears. *Why can't I ever think of the right thing to say?* she wondered.

"Yep," Ears continued, his smile returning. "I've been held back. It's not quite like half-back, but it'll have to do."

"This is my turn-off," Elise said, relieved that she wouldn't have to try and think of what to say anymore.

"Later!" Ears said, clicking on his tape and speeding down the sidewalk.

Elise watched, listening till the clatter of his skates took him out of sight. *Maybe Garren will have to stay after school tomorrow, too. And if he does, maybe Ears . . .*

"You know, I wouldn't mind trying a pair of those myself." Herbie glided through the air on imaginary skates. "Almost as graceful as cloud surfing."

"I don't think they come in solid gold," Elise laughed, remembering Herbie's gold teeth and gold spiral with his tiny gold pencil. She turned toward home, her smile fading. "Herbie, is there something wrong with me?"

"Like what?"

"Oh, I don't know. Maybe something with my brain."

"Your brain?" As he flew, Herbie pulled out his gold spiral and leafed through several pages. "Nope. In fact, no problems with any of your bodily functions." He stuffed the spiral back up his sleeve. "Why do you ask?"

"I can't ever seem to think of the right thing to say. All my words sound stupid in my ears. I'm never clever and quick. Especially when I want to be."

"Nonsense! You have a fine command of the French language."

"I speak English, Herbie."

"English! That's what I meant." Herbie flashed a sheepish grin. "Almost all humans get tongue-tied when they are in new or tense situations—or when they want to make a good impression. Like you did with Ears."

Elise felt herself blush. "He only walked me home because Garren had to stay after school."

"Right," Herbie said. "And you couldn't find the way by yourself."

Elise swiped at Herbie with her spiral notebook, but he was too quick for her. "He's just a friend of Garren's," she said, trying not to smile.

"Never lie to your guardian angel, kid," Herbie called from high above before disappearing into the treetops.

Good grief! Elise thought, glancing at the time on her watch. *I've got to get home.* Riley had promised to come over later, and Elise wanted to make sure her room looked perfect.

May my spoken words and unspoken thoughts be pleasing even to you, O Lord.
(Psalm 19:14 TLB)

39

Chapter
9

"Your room looks like something out of a Barbie house," Riley said. "All pink and white. Makes me want to run out and buy some cotton candy." She moved around the room, stopping before Elise's bookshelves long enough to scan the titles.

"I *like* pink and white," Elise said, an edge to her voice. "And so did my mom."

Riley held up both hands. "No offense intended. I've just never been surrounded by so much femininity before." She opened the lid of a carved box on Elise's dresser. "Any family jewels lurking in here?"

Quickly Elise picked up the box and held it to her. "Nothing much." *Just all I have left of my mother*, she thought. Some make-up. An old class ring. And a strand of pearls. Real ones. Elise remembered the way they looked around her mother's neck, all swirly and soft, like round drops of candlelight strung together.

Riley laughed. "My business-suit-and-sensible-shoes mother would probably freak out if I told her I wanted a Barbie-pink room. Your mom really liked this kind of stuff?"

Elise wanted to change the subject. She didn't want to talk about her mother. Or about what was in her jewelry box. Not yet.

"Are you going to sign up for the school newspaper?" Riley asked, plopping belly-first onto Elise's bed.

"I don't know."

"Do you like to write?"

"Sure. But I don't know if I could do newspaper stuff."

Riley rolled over on her back. "It's easy. Just all that *who, what, where, when,* and *why* stuff Miss Rosetti is always talking about. You get to interview interesting people and get into sports events free. The editor even lets you give up your lunch hour to staple and deliver copies. Almost more fun than one human being can stand."

"Oh, I don't know," Elise said, picking up Riley's tone. "I can stand more fun than the average human being."

"Good," Riley said, standing up and reaching for her book bag. "I'll see you at the organizational meeting tomorrow during homeroom. I need all the good writers I can get."

"*You* need?"

Riley turned to smile as she started down the stairs. "Yeah, I'm the editor. Don't be late!"

"Why do *I* have to do it?" Elise struggled to zip up her jacket. Her hands shook.

"Because you've been on the newspaper staff for a whole week now. Because it's a topic our readers want to know about. Because I'm the editor and I said so." Riley slammed her locker and turned to face Elise. "It's a cheerleading practice, not a lion's den. Now go make like a reporter. I've got to get to my cello lesson."

Elise headed toward the gym, her steps echoing in the empty hallway. A custodian pushed a huge dust mop along the floor.

"Girl reporter hot on the trail of a scoop!" Herbie was perched on the top of the row of lockers near the gym. He wore a tiny hat with a big PRESS card sticking in the band. He flew over to Elise. "I could get to like this newspaper stuff."

"Then why don't you do this interview?"

"Hey, it was your idea. And a good one! 'Cheerleading: A Behind-the-Scenes Look.'"

Elise sighed. It had seemed like a good idea when she'd suggested it to Riley. And it would give her a chance to spend time with Alissa and Dawn and some of the other "in's," as Herbie called them. But now . . . now she could feel the sweat forming on her palms, and her tongue seemed glued between her teeth.

Herbie flew in front of her and stopped to face her. "Listen, kid. What you're feeling is normal. Take a few deep breaths. Come on!"

Elise breathed in, feeling her lungs expand. The hall smelled like floor polish and chalk dust. Slowly she exhaled.

"Again!" Herbie said, his small chest rising and falling in time with hers. "Now, close your eyes and think about the questions you made up. You're ready for this! And a quick prayer always helps!"

From behind the double doors Elise could hear the chanting of cheers and the thud of feet. *Help me, God. I need to make a good impression* . . .

Just then the door burst open and in a cluster of

swirling ponytails and laughter, the girls headed for the drinking fountain.

"You're on, kid!" Herbie said, disappearing in a swirl of angel dust.

Elise cleared her throat. "Hi."

No response. They seemed to be in a world of their own, unaware of Elise standing with her spiral and pen, near the door.

"I think we should get saddle shoes. Red and white to match our uniforms," Dawn said in between slurps of water.

"Overkill," said Alissa matter-of-factly. "Basic white is best—but how about socks with red hearts on them?"

The others all began talking at once, taking sides, voicing the pros and cons of each choice.

"Excuse me," Elise said, louder this time. "I'm from *The Crusader*."

The girls looked at her with plainly puzzled expressions.

"The school newspaper. I'm here to do a story about cheerleading. Mrs. Sawyer said you were expecting me."

Suddenly Dawn broke into a hundred-watt smile. "Oops, I forgot to tell you guys. I promised our dear old sponsor we'd give our good friend Elise here an interview all about the difficult yet rewarding job of cheerleading."

Our friend Elise?

"Come inside," Dawn said, looping her arm through Elise's. "The gym will be just the proper setting. You writers get into setting, don't you?"

"Sure," Elise said, smiling back at Dawn. *Maybe this*

reporter stuff is just what I need to break into that "inner" circle!

I can do everything through him who gives me strength.

(Philippians 4:13)

Chapter  10

"Why do you always do that?"
Riley asked.

"Do what?" Elise plunged her straw deep into her chocolate shake.

"Watch my mouth when I talk. Makes me feel like I've got fungus growing on my teeth or something."

Elise felt her cheeks redden. "It's just . . . just a habit I have." Elise remembered when she was first learning to read lips—how hard she had to concentrate, the tears of frustration when she couldn't follow the conversation. She could almost hear her mother's voice. *Come on, pumpkin. You can do this. Why, a bright girl like you can do anything she sets her head to.* Now there was no need to read lips, but she was so used to watching every word.

"What we really need," Riley said, pulling Elise back into the present, "is something sensational. Stories that will make the kids *want* to read the school newspaper." She dunked her french fry into the tiny container of honey.

"You mean like 'UFO Spotted on White House

Lawn' or 'Baby Born with Two Heads'?" Elise asked, jabbing her straw into the corners of her cup for the last bit of shake.

"Let's try something with a little more credibility," Riley said.

"How about a 'Letters to the Editor' section? My dad's always writing letters to the editor of *The Chicago Tribune*."

"We tried that last year," Riley said, licking the last of the honey off her fingers. "All we got were complaints about homework and a suggestion that we make the restrooms coed."

Elise looked over Riley's shoulder at the back page of the newspaper the man in the next booth was reading. *PHANTOM OF THE OPERA TO MAKE NATIONAL TOUR* the headline read. "But what if this time you *knew* you'd get some good letters?"

"And how would I know that? Consult my crystal ball?"

"No, it could be an inside job. By an anonymous person, a sort of phantom who could write about all kinds of things. A critic of the system. A champion whose identity would keep your readers guessing."

Riley's eyes lit up. "A Robin Hood with a pen. Someone to champion the cause of the common kid."

"Who on your staff could do it?" Elise asked.

Riley smiled slightly as she wadded up her french fry package and tossed it onto the tray. "Only one person I know of."

"Who?"

"Somebody who's new, somebody who can take a fresh look at things we've been stepping over and walking around for years at Hinkle Creek."

47

"Good idea." Elise tossed her empty cup onto the tray.

Riley leaned across the table toward Elise. "Nobody can know. Nobody. If even one person besides us knows, it won't work."

"I won't tell," Elise said. "Who's the 'phantom'?"

"You," Riley said.

"Elise! Elise! Wait up!"

Elise turned to see Dawn running down the hall after her. She slowed her pace so Dawn could catch up.

"I just saw the newspaper article you wrote about me . . . I mean, about cheerleading. I was so-o-o impressed!"

"Thanks," Elise said. They walked together toward English class. *Come on now. This is what you've been waiting for. Here you are walking down the hall with one of the most popular girls in seventh grade. Think of something clever to say!* "Did the other girls like it, too?" Not clever.

"Loved it! L-O-V-E-D it!" Dawn said it like a cheer, and Elise couldn't be sure if she was serious or not.

Every few feet someone said "hi" to Dawn. Even eighth graders knew her. No one seemed to notice Elise. *I'll make a great phantom,* she thought. *I'm already invisible to everybody in the school.*

"Hey, Elise! How's life in seventh grade?" Garren waved from across the hall as he moved toward the gym. Elise smiled and waved back.

"You and Garren are pretty good friends, aren't you?" Dawn asked as they reached their classroom door.

"Yeah, I guess so."

"You aren't . . . you know . . . going with him or anything?"

Elise laughed. "Hardly! He lives next door to me, and we got to be pretty good friends when I was . . . when I first moved here." Elise wasn't ready to tell Dawn about her deafness. Not now. Maybe not ever.

"Oh, good!" Dawn giggled. "He's such a hunk, don't you think?"

Elise shrugged. "Sure. All that wrestling practice and weight lifting . . ."

But Dawn was gone, skittering across the room to whisper something to Alissa just as the bell rang to start class.

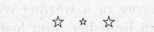

Each of you should look not only to your own interests, but also to the interests of others.
(Philippians 2:4)

Chapter

11

"I got a note from your gym teacher," Elise's dad said matter-of-factly, as if he were giving a sports score or a weather report.

Elise looked up from her meat loaf—and waited.

But it wasn't until he had cleaned his plate and poured himself a cup of coffee that he gave any more details.

"Seems you are not complying with the rules."

"I comply with all her rules!" Elise protested. "I wear those baggy shorts and stretched out T-shirts. I jump rope and run laps and take notes on those boring 'Origin of Sports' filmstrips."

Elise's dad was silent. The only sound was the clank of his spoon as he stirred milk into his coffee.

Why doesn't he say something? I hate his patient father routine! If mother were here, she'd understand. Elise tossed her fork onto her plate. "Okay, so there's one rule I don't think is fair. And I won't do it."

Her father raised one eyebrow. *"Won't?"*

"No," she said, her chin coming up in determination. "I won't take off all my clothes and shower naked in front of all those other girls. Not if it means staying in seventh grade until I'm forty!"

Slowly, Elise's father sipped his coffee. "Rules are rules. After all, you are all females."

Females? He makes us sound like specimens in some laboratory experiment.

"Daddy," Elise pleaded. "Gym class is awful. Not the class part, really. But afterward. The noise in the locker room is terrible—all that water sputtering and crashing onto the cement floor. And the girls' yells and squeals echoing endlessly. I know I'll go mad if I have to stand there stark naked in the middle of it all."

Elise shuddered, remembering how shocked she was the first time she had to change clothes in front of everybody. She hid behind her locker door, slipping her gym clothes on as she slid her school clothes off. How could these girls do it? But of course, Elise knew. They had sisters, shared the bathroom with their mother, had been to each other's houses to spend the night. They were comfortable with each other. *I'm a freak, still. I can hear, but I can't fit in. I'll never be like them. I'll never catch up from those years. Those silent, wonderful years.* It startled Elise to realize that she had actually, for a minute, longed for the time when she had been deaf.

Her father cleared his throat. "Staying in seventh grade until you are forty is not an option. Perhaps you would like to talk to Mrs. Gillum?"

"Mrs. Gillum? What does she have to do with any of this?"

Her father toyed with the end of his spoon. "This is awkward for me, Elise. What do I know about bringing up a young woman? Mrs. Gillum said any time I needed a woman's touch . . ."

Elise got up and began clearing the table. "I don't need Mrs. Gillum or any other woman's touch. I'll take care of gym class myself." The grinding whir of the garbage disposal vibrated the kitchen air, and Elise tried not to shrink from the sound.

Her father's chair scraped across the floor as he rose from the table. When he passed Elise, he paused to place an awkward hand on her shoulder. "Be a good girl, now."

Elise again turned on the garbage disposal and stood, unflinchingly this time, as it pulverized her uneaten meat loaf.

Children, obey your parents in the Lord, for this is right. Honor your father and mother.
(Ephesians 6:1–2)

Chapter 12

"I hate Mrs. Sawyer," Elise said later to Herbie as she sat on her bed doing homework.

"No, you don't."

"Well, I hate gym class."

"Hating a subject is not the same as hating a person. Hate is as powerful as it is evil."

"And I hate rules. I'm sick to death of them."

Herbie chuckled. "I have yet to meet one of your species who enjoyed being told what to do! But imagine life without rules."

Elise stopped underlining verbs in her English sentences and looked up. "What do you mean?"

"No one would stop at stop signs. Or pay taxes. No one would obey speed laws. Rioting and looting would be everyday occurrences. Soon the whole planet would be mayhem."

"I'd never thought of rules in the big sense. I guess I don't hate all rules, just stupid ones that do nobody any good."

"Like showers after gym class?"

Elise slammed her notebook shut. "Everybody always tells me what to do. Why have a brain if adults never let you use it?"

"You use your brain every day! Just slamming that book took impulses running from your brain to your arm." Herbie flew down and nudged Elise's grammar book with his bare toe. "Remember when you first began learning how to do subjects and verbs?"

Elise nodded. "Fourth grade. It seemed impossible! They all just looked like words to me."

Herbie nodded. "But you did learn the difference, by *practicing*. And every year you've been able to do more advanced grammar because you have that foundation to build on. That's the way it is with the rules in your life now, too."

"What do you mean?"

"Well, learning to abide by things like school attendance policies and soccer practice schedules prepares you for other 'rules' in your life—for showing up for work on time and getting your driver's license and keeping your checks from bouncing."

Elise gathered up her books and put them in her book bag. "It's not the same, Herbie."

Herbie sighed. "Listen, kid. Everything abides by rules. Even nature. Summer and winter, roses dying and eggs hatching. It all operates under his jurisdiction."

"But what if there's one rule you just can't live with?" Elise turned to face Herbie. "Hey, Herbie! Couldn't you . . . do something? Maybe break the pipes in the locker room for the rest of the year? Or give Mrs. Sawyer a nightmare that would make her never assign showers again?"

54

"The Management doesn't look kindly on that kind of tampering," Herbie said, shaking his head. "Besides, you say you want a chance to use that brain of yours. Here it is! You can figure this out—with a little help."

"From you?" Elise asked.

But Herbie had disappeared, leaving behind the tinkling sound of wind chime laughter.

"Showering after P.E. is no big deal," Riley said the next afternoon as she and Elise worked in the computer lab.

"Shhh!" Elise looked around to see if anybody else had heard.

Riley laughed. "We're the only ones left in here. The editor and her trusty companion, proofreading copy."

Elise punched in the "spell-check" feature and waited as the computer scanned for errors. "Maybe it's no big deal for you, but it's a plenty big deal for me." Elise paused to correct a misspelling. "I . . . I can't take all my clothes off like that. I feel everybody is looking at me. And laughing."

Riley clicked off her machine. "Here's how it works." She put her hands on her knees and leaned toward Elise. "You go straight from your gym shorts and shirt into your towel. Nothing shows above or below, except those long legs of yours. Once you get in the shower room, all you have to do is paddle around in the water a little and squeal. Make sure your towel gets wet. Old lady Sawyer never pays close attention. A few drops on your arms, a shiver as you pass by her office, and a damp towel to toss in the pile. And presto! Happy teacher, happy parent."

Elise finished her proofing and filed the story onto the hard drive. Then she leaned back and looked at Riley. "It just might work."

Riley stood up and began buttoning her parka. "Might work? It's been working for decades. Even my mom used that cunning bit of fraud when she faced the terrors of teenage group showers."

Your mom. What else will my mom not be around to tell me? Elise thought about her dad's offer of Mrs. Gillum. *Never!*

Listen to advice and accept instruction, and in the end you will be wise.
                    (Proverbs 19:20)

Chapter 13

"We've never had an issue of the paper generate this much excitement before," Riley said, noisily slurping the last of her milk from its carton.

Elise looked around the cafeteria. At almost every table, kids were holding up *The Crusader* and pointing to the last page.

"Who do you suppose 'The Phantom' is?" Elise heard one girl at the next table ask.

"I'm sure it's a boy," her friend replied.

"How do you know?"

"It just *sounds* like a boy!"

Elise smiled as she bit into her hamburger. It was a good article. All about cafeteria food. Some of it was funny, like the part about the pet pigs they kept in back to eat all the food the kids left on their plates. But some of it was serious, too. Elise had taken a sample week's menu and showed how much fat was in it. Even suggested a few new items for the cafeteria to serve— like frozen yogurt and carrot-raisin salad. The piece had ended with The Phantom challenging the cook to a duel: day-old hot dog buns at thirty paces.

"Later," Riley said as she picked up her tray. "I have to finish my Spanish before next period." She bent close to Elise's ear as she stood. "And be thinking about where The Phantom will strike next," she whispered.

After Riley left, Elise sat looking around the cafeteria. It didn't seem so noisy now. And she knew lots of kids. A high-pitched giggle made her look to the far corner. Dawn.

"Pet pigs in the back room!" she squealed. "That must be where Melinda goes between meals."

All the girls around her laughed and looked in the direction of a chubby girl sitting alone at the next table. She bent her head lower toward her tray and ate without looking up.

"Not funny," Herbie said, appearing next to Elise.

Elise picked up her tray and walked toward the trash cans. "I remember in second grade, how the kids would tease me about not hearing well. They called me 'deaf and dumb'—even though I always had the highest grades in spelling." She placed her tray on the conveyer belt and then stepped into the hallway.

"You humans," Herbie said. "Always trying to make yourselves look better by making someone else look worse. Reminds me of chickens."

"Chickens?" Elise wrinkled up her nose.

Herbie nodded. "The pecking order. The big chicken will peck a smaller one. And he will peck an even littler one. And so on and so on. In fact, if a chicken is too tiny or too weak, the chickens will all get together and peck it to death."

"Sick!" Elise said, just as Melinda pushed open the

58

door and, after looking both ways, hurried alone down the hallway.

"Maybe," Herbie mused. "But I've always thought that's probably why he didn't give you humans beaks."

Every other Friday the newspaper came out. And every time, the letter from The Phantom was the talk of the school. By Thanksgiving, the mystery writer had achieved celebrity status.

"I wish I knew who The Phantom was," Dawn said to Elise just before English class.

"Why?" Elise asked.

"Because," Dawn said, "everybody thinks I know all the important people in school." She twirled a stray stand of hair. "It's, like, expected of me, you know?" She laughed nervously. "Besides, I'd like to invite him to my party this weekend."

"Him?" Riley said as she paused beside Elise's desk.

"Or her," Dawn shrugged. "I personally couldn't bear to be a nobody! What a pity to be popular and not get to take advantage of it!"

The bell signaled the beginning of class, but Elise couldn't concentrate on vocabulary lists. She kept thinking about what Dawn had said. *What a pity to be popular and not get to take advantage of it.*

Do to others as you would have them do to you.
(Luke 6:31)

59

Chapter 14

"Coming to my wrestling meet tomorrow?" Garren tossed Elise the ball, and she dribbled toward the hoop and shot. The ball arched up and bounced off the rim of the backboard attached to Garren's garage.

"Too much violence for me," she teased. "All those bloody noses and broken bones."

Garren rebounded and slam dunked. "I promise not to crush anyone's spine if you come."

They played their one-on-one for another ten minutes without talking. Then Garren hugged the ball to his chest and said, "Seriously. It's time you came to something in the gym. And wrestling meets aren't nearly as noisy as basketball games."

Elise pulled the hood of her sweatshirt up against the chill of the wind. Garren understood her so well, better than anybody. Except maybe Herbie. What would Garren think if she told him she had a guardian angel?

"Think fast!" Garren said, whizzing the ball toward her.

Elise instinctively grabbed it and made a fast break

for the basket. "Two points!" she cheered. "Now let's quit. I'm ahead."

Elise sat staring into the fireplace, enjoying the first fire of the season. Her dad had gone to mail some letters, and she had the whole, cozy room to herself. Finally, she was beginning to thaw out from the game with Garren.

"You really should, you know." Herbie hovered in front of the fireplace, roasting a marshmallow on a long gold fork.

"Should what?" Elise asked, settling into the pillows on the couch.

"Go to Garren's wrestling meet. He's your friend, and he wants you to go."

"I don't like wrestling meets."

"You've never even been!"

"I've never been lion hunting, but I know I wouldn't like it," Elise said, picking up a magazine and hoping Herbie would let the idea alone.

"Nonsense!" Herbie huffed, popping the marshmallow into his mouth. "D two tings ave nuttin in cmn."

Elise laughed. "I guess even angels can't talk with their mouths full."

Herbie swallowed. "Sorry." He popped the fork up his sleeve and flew over beside Elise. "Seriously, kid. New experiences are part of God's plan for humans. That's how they learn and grow. It's time you tried a few new things. A few new, *noisy* things."

Elise shuddered. "It'll be worse than even the locker room. I know it."

Herbie sat down and folded his arms. "You'll never know until you try. Fear of the unknown is almost always worse than the actual experience. Why, take those Israelites a few years ago, when Moses led them out of Egypt."

"A *few* years ago?" Elise said.

Herbie waved the comment aside. "The fact remains. What kept them from the Promised Land—and ticked off God pretty bad—was their fear. They could have taken those giants from Canaan. A whole squadron of angels had been assigned to help them. But . . . nooooo. Instead, they wandered in the wilderness like lost salamanders for forty years."

"If I decide to go to the wrestling meet," Elise said, "will I get a squadron of angels to help me?"

Herbie stood up and puffed out his chest. "No need! Super Herbie is on the job." He took off and swooped, Superman style, around the room.

Just then, her dad opened the front door. Herbie barely missed his hat, and Elise tried to hide her giggle behind her hand.

"Something amusing?" her dad asked, taking off his coat and shaking flakes of snow to the floor.

"Not really," Elise said. "I've just decided to go to Garren's wrestling meet tomorrow, and I was thinking about how much fun it might be."

☆　☆　☆

Do not be anxious about anything, but in everything, by prayer and petition, with thanksgiving, present your requests to God.
(Philippians 4:6)

Chapter

15

The whole place smelled like popcorn and mildew. It was an odd combination that made Elise's nose twitch and her stomach lurch. She sat alone on the bleachers. Not even Herbie was in sight.

Below her, on the mats, wrestlers in bright team sweats practiced takedowns, did push-ups, arched against imaginary opponents. Elise was relieved that, so far, the noise was tolerable. At first the thuds and grunts of the wrestlers startled her, their sounds echoing eerily off the high ceilings. Garren had told her about that. "Things sound worse than they really are," he'd said that morning when she told him she was coming. "So don't get freaked. Besides," he'd added, grinning. "We're all too tough to hurt!"

Elise saw Dawn and a group of her friends come in. They sat near the floor, sharing a box of popcorn. Elise watched them with envy. Sometimes she thought Dawn wanted to be friends. Other times she acted like Elise was a piece of furniture. *If she knew I was The Phantom* . . . Elise thought.

"Ah, the thrill of human competition!" Herbie sha-dowboxed an imaginary opponent in midair.

"This your first wrestling meet, too, Herbie?" Elise asked.

"Humph! Are you kidding? You forget how long I've been around. I remember the Olympics when they were a newfangled idea." He turned to survey the mats. "Still, there is a grand feel to these competitions."

"I just hope it's not too noisy . . ."

"Who are you talking to?" Garren plopped down beside Elise. The bleacher seemed to give under his weight.

"Um . . . nobody. Myself."

"Glad you made it!" Garren said. "I was afraid you'd chicken out."

"Actually, I only came for the popcorn," Elise said, smiling.

"Then let me get you some!"

Before Elise could protest, Garren stood up and—taking the bleachers two at a time—jogged out to the lobby. Elise saw Dawn and her friends speak to him when he walked past. Soon he was back with a huge tub of buttered popcorn.

"Well, this ought to last me . . . for the next two years!" Elise laughed.

"You're welcome," Garren said, taking a handful off the top.

"Will it start soon?"

Garren nodded. "One of the buses from Park Forest was late, so weigh-ins were delayed. But everything's almost ready."

"Are you going to win?"

"Is the sun going to rise tomorrow? Just make sure you're watching. I don't want to get a ten-second pin and have you miss it."

"Hi! Mind if I join you two?"

Elise looked up to see Dawn. "Uh, no. Of course not. I mean, we don't mind." Elise picked up the tub of popcorn to make room for Dawn.

But instead of sitting next to Elise, Dawn sat down next to Garren. "Tough match tonight?" she asked, staring up into his face.

"They're all tough." He turned back to Elise. "Catch you later. Don't forget to yell for me."

Elise smiled. "Sure thing . . . what was your name again?"

Garren gave her hair a playful pull and ran down to the mat.

"What a hunk!" Dawn squealed, closing her eyes and crinkling up her nose. "I hope he doesn't hurt that gorgeous body."

"I wouldn't worry about Garren," Elise said. She waited for Dawn to rejoin her friends, but she seemed in no hurry to leave. "Want some popcorn?"

"Sure!" Dawn said, carefully picking out the butteryest kernels.

The gym was filling up, and the noise level was rising. The voices seemed to blend in a buzz that made Elise's head swim. She took a deep breath, fought down the feeling of panic. She wiped her sweaty palms on her jeans. *I can't let Dawn see me like this!* Slowly, she separated the sounds. Feet stomping up the bleachers. Kids calling out to each other. The whispers of clusters of friends. Coaches yelling instructions. She could deal with it. All of it. One piece at a time.

One by one the matches progressed. Hinkle Creek was behind. And then, finally, the announcer's voice rang out.

"And at 145, wrestling for Hinkle Creek Middle School, defending conference champion—G-a-rren Gillum!" The gym burst into applause. Elise fought to keep from covering her ears against the rush of sound.

Garren faced his opponent, and a look Elise had never seen before came on his face. His jaw was clinched; his eyes, cold. Elise knew that because Garren was defending conference champ everyone was out to beat him. Pin him. The ref blew his whistle—a shrill, sharp sound that made Elise shudder. "Get 'um, Gillum!" she yelled.

"Go, Garren!" Dawn echoed beside her.

His opponent shot, but it was shallow, and Garren ended up on top. But when the move stalled, the ref brought them back to the center of the mat. This time Garren's opponent shot—and scored a solid takedown.

"He's behind!" Dawn wailed.

Elise ignored her. Garren had warned her not to take her eyes off the mat for even a second. "Things happen fast in wrestling," he'd said. And he was right! Garren strained against his opponent and, in a flash, was on his feet. Escape! Garren's point! Then, grasping his opponent around the waist, Garren worked for a four-point move. Elise could see his muscles strain as he brought him up . . . up . . . up and over! *Thud!* A scramble of arms and legs. Then Garren was on top, working the half. His opponent was on his back, gasping. Elise realized she was digging her nails into her palm. "Come on, Garren!" she yelled. Garren tugged the boy's head up, forced the shoulder blades into the mat. Deeper. Deeper.

"I can't look," Dawn mumbled into her hands.

Whap! The ref's hand slapped the mat. Pin! Garren had won with a pin! Slowly, both boys walked back to the center of the mat. And when the ref raised Garren's hand in victory, Elise found herself a happy part of the noisy whooping and thunderous applause.

Cast all your anxiety on him, because he cares for you.

(1 Peter 5:7)

68

Chapter 16

"Do you have a picture of your mom?"

Elise looked up from the newspaper article she was clipping. All around them the floor was cluttered with copies of *The Chicago Tribune* that she and Riley were using to get articles for their social studies projects.

"Sure," Elise said softly.

"I want to see it."

Even after all these months, Elise still couldn't get used to the way Riley just blurted out whatever she thought and whatever she wanted. Elise went to a drawer in her dresser and pulled out a worn picture album. The first picture was of her mom. It had been taken only a few weeks before she'd died. A suntanned woman with green eyes smiled into the camera. The wind was blowing strands of her honey blond hair across one cheek. Elise handed the opened album to Riley.

"Here. My mom." Elise wanted to say more, but what? What could you say when the person you loved most on earth was only a photograph? How could you talk to someone like Riley, someone whose mother was jetting around the country, about what it was like to walk across your mother's grave?

"She's pretty," Riley said. "Looks a lot like you."

Elise reached for the album, but Riley held on. "Let's play truth and swear," she said.

"What's that?" Elise asked.

"I ask you a question and you have to tell me the truth. Then you get to ask me something. And we both swear to never tell anyone else what's said. Fair enough?"

Elise sat down on the floor across from Riley. She wasn't sure she wanted to tell Riley all about her past, but, still—there were things about Riley she'd been dying to know. "Okay," she said.

"Great. I'll start." Riley looked again at the picture. "How did your mom die?"

Elise swallowed. She knew this would be Riley's first question. She'd answered it dozens of times in the past three years, had memorized an answer that let her deliver information without feeling so much pain. "It was in July. The summer I was ten. A truck full of grain ran a stop sign and hit her. She was killed instantly." There. That was it. Like a newspaper report. *On July 25, Desila Renee Daum was struck by a loaded grain truck when its driver failed to yield at a stop sign. She was pronounced dead on arrival . . .*

"What was the funeral like?"

Elise shrugged. "Awful, what I remember of it. I was kind of numb. I remember lots of people coming and going. And the kitchen counter piled with food. The funeral home was filled with people. I could see them crying. But once and awhile someone would laugh—

and I knew that they were remembering something clever my mother had said. I kept waiting for her to sit up in the casket and say, 'Surprise! Only kidding!' My mother was a great joker, always playing pranks. She could have been a stand-up comedian." Elise took a deep breath. "The days after the funeral were worse. I thought Father would go crazy. He just stood outside and cried. Wouldn't eat. I don't even think he slept. Every afternoon I used to lie on the floor in my mother's closet. It smelled so much like her! I'd pretend she was just gone to the grocery store . . ." Elise swallowed hard and squinched her eyes against the tears. *Oh, Mother! Why did you have to leave me now, just when I need you so?*

"Your turn," Riley said.

Elise opened her eyes. "Where did you get the name 'Riley'?"

Riley laughed. "The number-one question! My folks are poetry freaks, especially my dad. So when Mom got pregnant, they wanted to name the baby after their favorite Indiana poet: James Whitcomb Riley. And when that baby turned out to be a girl, they decided to go ahead with their plan anyway. So . . . my name is Whitcomb Riley Blohm."

"Whitcomb?" Elise asked.

Riley shook her head. "Now you know why 'Riley' doesn't sound so bad to me." Riley leafed through the photo album. Too late Elise realized she'd stopped in front of last year's group school picture—taken at the hearing impaired school. "Where's this? You went to a private school last year?"

"Well . . . sort of."

"A parochial school? A prep school? What?"

71

Elise took a big breath. "A hearing impaired school."

Riley laughed. "But why?"

"I was deaf."

Riley let out a low whistle. "Whoa, aren't you the little secret keeper! Were you born deaf? How come you can hear now?"

Elise knew Riley was asking more than her share of questions, but it would feel good to get it all out and never have to talk about it again.

"I was probably six when I first noticed it," she said. "Some days it would seem like all the sounds were wrapped in cotton. I can remember when I was eight and practicing for my first piano recital. I could feel the ivories under my finger tips, but the melodies were broken, somehow. Father always accused me of day-dreaming if I didn't hear what he said. And some days I *could* hear! But those days became fewer and fewer. In third grade I used to hope the teacher would write the assignment on the board so I could read it. I was embarrassed to admit I couldn't hear." Elise cleared her throat, braced herself to tell the hard part. "Finally, Mother began home-schooling me. Father seemed relieved not to have to deal with my teachers anymore. Mother and I learned sign just for fun, at first. But as the sounds became fewer, more blurred, we depended on it whenever we went to the grocery store or for walks. She helped me learn to read lips, too."

"So that's why you always stare at people's mouths when they talk!" Riley said.

Elise nodded quickly. "Then . . . then came the accident. Father was in a daze for months. I tried to keep up my studies by myself, but it was no use. When summer came, that first summer after her death, I thought he'd go crazy. Roaming around the house. Standing for hours in Mother's flower garden. Then, suddenly, we were moving. 'A fresh start,' he called it. A new job for him . . . a new school for me. But a school for . . . deaf children."

"Too weird," Riley whispered. "I bet Hinkle Creek seems like noise city to you."

Elise nodded. "Especially at first. The cafeteria and locker room were the worst."

"So, how did you get your hearing back?"

Elise smiled. "Isn't it my turn to ask a question?"

"Aw, come on!" Riley groaned. "Don't stop now. Something tells me this is the best part!"

Elise continued. "The audiologist who tested me that first day at the hearing impaired school seemed surprised when I told him I'd never been to a hearing doctor. Just Doc Smythe who always gave me this horrible tasting elixir for my colds and yellow drops for my earaches. He sent a note to Father. Suggested I see a specialist. But Father can be stubborn. It had taken him a long time to admit I really couldn't hear. It took him months to admit I needed to see a specialist. But finally, early last summer, we went to Boston. I had an operation, a 'micro-surgery' they called it. And I could hear! I remember waking up in the hospital to the sound of trays clinking outside my door. It was the sweetest sound I'd ever heard!"

"Elise! Elise!" her father called from the bottom of the steps. "Have you seen today's *Tribune*?"

Riley held up the first page of the issue, with a big hole where the lead story had been. She stuck her face through the opening. "News flash: Crazed professor pulverizes daughter's friend."

"Part of it, Dad . . ." Elise called back, the laughter rippling through her answer. *Friend.* It had a nice sound to it.

☆　☆　☆

He will . . . fill your mouth with laughter.
(Job 8:21)

Chapter 17

"My favorite time of year!" Herbie crooned, waltzing around the ceramic Christmas tree that sat on a table in front of the window.

"I wish it were Daddy's favorite time of year," Elise said gloomily. "Then we could have a real tree and lots of presents."

"Christmas isn't just about presents," Herbie said.

"I know, but when Mom was alive . . ." Elise turned away from the tiny, snowcapped tree. This was the third Christmas without her mother, but to Elise the pain was new every year.

"Hey, kid," Herbie said, flying over and perching on the arm of the couch. "Want to make some cookies or something?"

Elise sighed. "Maybe the smell of baking will help get Daddy in the Christmas mood." Just then the phone rang.

"Don't talk long!" Herbie said, flying toward the kitchen. "I'll start getting out the ingredients!"

"Hello?" Elise said into the receiver.

"Hi, Lisey. Is this snow Christmasy or what?"

Lisey? "Uh, yeah. Real Christmasy," Elise said, looking out the window, where fresh snow was falling. Who was this? No one ever called but Riley. And sometimes Garren.

"We just finished cheerleading practice, and my shoes are totally soaked from walking home in this!"

It was Dawn! "Yeah, I bet." *Why is she calling me? Why can't I think of anything to say?*

"Soon it'll be time for the student council Christmas dance."

Elise wanted to ask what Christmas dance, but she knew that wasn't the thing to say.

"So, do you have a date yet?" Dawn asked.

A date? "Um . . . not yet," Elise said, trying to sound as if she expected to get one any minute.

"What about Garren?" There was a funny tone to Dawn's voice.

"I told you—we're just friends."

Dawn giggled. "Well, I wouldn't mind if he was *my* best friend!"

Silence. *What do other girls talk about on the phone?* Elise wondered.

"What about that boy I see you with sometimes?" Dawn continued. "The one who's always playing tapes."

"Ears?"

Dawn giggled again. "Must be! He's a friend of Garren's, too, isn't he?"

"Yes," Elise answered.

"Maybe he'll take you."

Elise imagined Ears taking her to the dance, showing up in a suit and tie—and Rollerblades. "I doubt it!"

76

"Maybe if he could double with Garren . . . if Garren was taking one of your friends."

Elise tried to imagine Riley with Garren.

"You'd like that, wouldn't you?" Dawn asked.

Elise thought about it. A dance. With big Christmas trees and fancy dresses. "Yes, I would," she answered honestly.

"Leave the rest to me!" Dawn said, just before she put the receiver down.

Elise held the buzzing phone away from her ear. *Now what does she mean by that?*

"Where's the chocolate chips?" Herbie yelled from the kitchen.

"In the freezer. But you'd better let me get them . . . you'll frostbite your wings!" Elise hurried to the kitchen to start her Christmas baking.

Elise was surprised the next day to see posters for the Christmas dance everywhere—on the glass wall of the cafeteria, posted outside the office, on the hallway bulletin board. Someone had even stuck one up in the girls' bathroom.

"Have you ever been to the Christmas dance?" Elise asked Riley as they stapled the Christmas issue of *The Crusader*.

"Nope. Couldn't go last year—no sixth graders allowed. Very big stuff. No little squirts admitted."

Elise pushed the stapler down on a stack of pages. "Are you going this year?"

Riley stopped and looked at her. "You mean, by myself?"

Elise shrugged. "I thought you might have a date or something."

"Actually," Riley said, straightening the stacks, "Prince Charming sent his falcon with a message that he was having his steed shod that night and wouldn't be able to make it."

Elise looked at Riley. Always the smart comment. Did she want to go? Would she like to wear a fancy dress? Elise had never seen Riley wear a dress, not even when her project had taken first place in the all-city science fair and there'd been a reception for the school board.

"I think The Phantom outdid *himself* this time, don't you?" Riley asked, counting the papers into homeroom piles.

Elise smiled. "It's one of my personal favorites." In his letter this time, The Phantom had complained about how too much emphasis was put on gifts between people, especially from kids to teachers. So he had suggested giving the money you'd spend on a teacher to the Salvation Army. The last part of the article listed things you could give your teachers that wouldn't cost much. A gradebook with the grades already filled in. Mouthwash. A tape of yourself burping songs from the sixties. The kids were going to love it! *Too bad they don't know it's me. But if they knew, if the mystery was gone, would they still think it was such great stuff?*

"I think that guy is trying to get your attention," Riley said, pointing toward the big glass window of the library. Ears was smiling and motioning toward Elise. "Go ahead. I can finish up here."

Ears held open the door for Elise. "Get the paper all done?"

"Almost," she said.

"So what did The Phantom write about this week?" he asked as they walked toward the gym.

"Top secret. You know the whole staff is sworn to silence until the papers are out," Elise replied.

"Right," Ears said, banging his head in mock frustration. "How could I forget a top-level thing like that?" Elise laughed. "Speaking of the Christmas dance," Ears said, stepping in front of Elise and turning to face her.

Elise stood still. She could hear the pounding of her heart. "We weren't speaking of the Christmas dance."

"Well, we are now. Want to go with me?" Ears said it fast, like he was afraid he wouldn't get it out.

A date. My first date. "Sure."

"That's okay," Ears said, shifting his books and walking down the hall. "I understand. If you change your mind . . ." He was several steps in front of Elise when he turned around. "What did you say?"

Elise smiled. "I said 'sure.' I'd like to go with you."

"Wait till Garren hears this!"

"Garren?"

"Yeah. He said if you'd go with me, he'd take your best friend and we'd double."

"Riley?" Elise asked, hardly able to believe her ears.

"No," Ears said. "Dawn."

☆ ⋆ ☆

We have renounced secret and shameful ways; we do not use deception.
(2 Corinthians 4:2)

79

Chapter 18

"Are you sure it'll be all right?" Elise asked, holding the emerald green taffeta dress up in front of the mirror.

"It will be perfect! Trust me. I've seen everything from Cleopatra's headpieces to the president's wife's inaugural ball gown. You need your black patent leather shoes with the bows . . ." Herbie flew into Elise's closet and began rummaging through shoe boxes.

If only Mother were here. She'd know what I should wear, Elise thought.

Herbie emerged holding one shoe, his halo crooked and his robe rumpled. "Whew! Now if I can just find the other one . . ." He dove back into the closet after dropping the shoe at Elise's feet.

She whirled again in front of the mirror. It *was* a lovely dress, and she'd only worn it once. Last Christmas at Aunt Wanda's wedding. Her third wedding. "When I get married, it's going to be forever and forever," she promised the figure in the mirror.

"Well now, that's certainly good news," Herbie said,

dropping the other shoe in front of Elise and plopping down on top of the dresser. "Divorce was never part of the Boss's plan for couples. But he sure sees a lot of it lately!"

"Like Garren's mom and dad."

"Ah," Herbie sighed. "I remember that divorce well!"

Elise pulled her hair up and stared into the mirror. The dress made her eyes look even more green. That was good, wasn't it? But it made her cheeks look pale. She walked to the dresser and carefully opened the carved box sitting on top.

"Your treasures," Herbie said. It was more a statement than a question. He leaned over to look inside.

"Sort of." Elise reached for her mother's blush and lipstick. She took them out and held them, reverently, in the palm of her hand. She could almost see her mom swiping the big brush with blush across her high cheekbones, lightly running the lipstick across her lips. "Every lady needs a little color," she'd say, laughing.

"No, I don't think she'd mind at all," Herbie said.

Elise smiled. Herbie always knew what she was thinking. She placed the cosmetics back into the box. From a small drawer she took out tiny, sparkly earrings. They, too, were from Aunt Wanda's wedding. She clipped them onto her ears and tilted her head from side to side, watching the rhinestones glisten in the light. "I wish Dawn would come over and look at my outfit, but I haven't even talked to her since that phone call. Every time I see her at school, she's surrounded by all these kids and seems . . . too busy to talk."

"Why don't you ask Riley to come over and look at your dress? She is your best friend, isn't she?"

Elise slipped the dress back on the hanger. "I guess so." *But Dawn told Ears she was my best friend. Why?*

"It's pretty obvious why, kid."

Elise sat down on the bed. Sometimes Herbie's mind reading was pretty annoying. "Maybe she wants to be my best friend. Is that so hard to believe?"

"You tell me. Does she act like a best friend?"

Elise thought about how she'd tried to talk to Dawn before English class that day, but Dawn had only waved and hurried on by with Alissa. She hadn't returned Elise's phone call from yesterday. And she had never once saved Elise a place at her table in the lunchroom. "So why did she say that?"

"Dawn's a crafty one. Always looking out for herself. She's using you, kid."

"Using me?"

"To get to Garren."

"That's not true! She wants to be my friend! She *is* my friend. And don't you say bad things about her!"

Herbie held up his hands. "Whoa, kid. Let's not get emotional. I've never quite understood those strong emotions you humans are so fond of."

Elise realized she still had on the shiny earrings. She walked to the dresser and plopped them into the jewelry box. Then she looked Herbie in the eye and said, "Excuse me. I'm going to go call my *friend* Dawn."

"She's not home!" Herbie called as Elise flounced down the steps.

"What do you mean you're going to the Christmas dance?" Elise looked at her dad in disbelief.

"I'm going to be a chaperon," he said, clicking the remote control of the television. "I thought it would be the proper way to meet some of your friends and see where you spend your days."

"Please say you're joking!" But even as she said it, Elise knew what a feeble hope it was. Her dad never joked.

"I'm quite in earnest, I assure you. Now, shall I wear the brown suit or the gray?" He found a documentary on whales and settled back to watch.

What if the whole evening is a disaster? Elise thought. *My dad there spying on me. Ears probably stepping on my feet with every dance. And Dawn. Would she be friendly? Was Herbie right about her?*

Elise was beginning to feel like Cinderella—just after the clock struck midnight.

Commit to the Lord whatever you do, and your plans will succeed.

(Proverbs 16:3)

Chapter 19

Smoke. Everywhere smoke. A cold, blue smoke that made Elise shiver. Mist tingled on her face, and a sense of fear gripped her. Where was she? And then she saw it. The figure. It turned toward her, a billowy hood hiding its face. A long, thin hand motioned her forward. Elise tried to move, but her feet felt nailed to the floor. She struggled. The figure turned away. "No, wait! I'm coming!" Suddenly Elise's feet were loose, and she ran through the foggy dampness. Her chest ached. Every breath was a searing pain. The figure stopped and turned to face her. It seemed impatient. Again it motioned. "Yes!" Elise yelled, every word tearing at her lungs. "I'm coming!" But she felt as though she were on a treadmill, going nowhere. The figure moved into the smoke and disappeared. "No!" Elise screamed.

When she woke, she was crying. With a shaking hand, Elise brushed away the tears. That dream. That stupid dream. Always the same thing. Who was the figure? Where was it going? And why was it so important that she follow?

Elise clicked on the light beside her bed. 2 A.M. Wind was rattling her windowpane, whistling through the limbs of the bare trees outside in the backyard.

"Rough night, kid?" Herbie yawned and stretched.

"I've had better." Elise clicked off the light and snuggled into the covers. "What does it mean, Herbie?"

"Your dream?" A soft light glowed as Herbie landed on Elise's pillow. "Dreams have been around for as long as you humans have. Sometimes God uses them to tell people things. It was in a dream that God told Pharaoh a seven-year famine was coming."

"And an angel appeared in a dream telling Joseph to take Mary for his wife," Elise said, remembering the Christmas story.

Wind chime laughter danced around the room. "What a time that was! All heaven was atwitter with excitement. God's son, being born to a virgin. So many details to attend to—a star to follow and the angelic messengers to send to the shepherds and a sure-footed donkey to provide . . ."

"But what about my dream? That's not from God, is it?"

Herbie was quiet for a minute. "That's one you make up yourself, kid. Out of your subconscious, where all your worries and fears come to life."

"My stress dream, right?" Elise pulled the covers tighter.

"Bingo."

"Herbie," she hesitated, not sure she wanted to ask the next question. "Who's the figure? Why do I feel such an aching need to follow it?"

Herbie sighed, and the quiet glow around him

dimmed for just a minute. "Think hard, kid. You know."

Elise licked her lips. Her throat felt suddenly dry, and her chest tight, like in the dream. "It's Mother, isn't it?"

Herbie nodded. "Yes."

"And I'm trying to get to her," Elise continued, "but I can't."

"You have the dream whenever you feel most strongly your need for her advice or comfort. Like just before school started."

"Or now. Just before my first date, my first dance." Elise lay listening to the ticking of her clock and the cold whistle of the wind. "I'll never catch her in the dream, will I, Herbie? I'll never be with her again. Not ever."

"Never's a long time!" Herbie said, brightening. "In fact, you humans have no idea how long *ever* really is. Eternity is forever and forever. And that's how long you'll be with your mother in heaven."

"Really?" Elise asked, raising up on one elbow and looking at Herbie.

"Angels never lie! Especially about heaven."

"Tell me about heaven, Herbie."

Herbie smiled. And Elise had never seen him glow brighter. "It's a great place! The walls are filled with emeralds and sapphires and lots of other jewels. The streets are even shinier gold than my teeth! And the gates are made of solid pearl."

"Pearl?" Elise asked. "Like the pearls in Mom's necklace?"

"Only bigger and better. *Everything* in heaven is bigger and better! And everywhere is white, warm light—a thousand times brighter than the sun. God himself lights up the whole place. It's better than fireworks. Best of all, there's no pain or sadness. Ever. And forever." Herbie sighed. "Let's change the subject, kid. I'm starting to get homesick."

"Why did she have to die, Herbie?"

"Because it's the way with humans," Herbie said. "Because everything is part of a big plan that no one but the Boss really understands. And because death is the only way to get to the really good stuff: peace and eternal life and a chance to audition for heaven's choir."

Elise closed her eyes and smiled, imagining her mother in heaven. In the alto section. Telling jokes in between songs.

And as Herbie hummed *Silent Night*, Elise drifted off to sleep.

I am the resurrection and the life. He who believes
in me will live, even though he dies.
(John 11:25)

Chapter

20

Elise leaned into the mirror, checking her makeup. The blush brought a hint of color to her cheeks, and the pale pink lipstick was just right. She smoothed the green taffeta of her dress.

"Smashing!" Herbie said, eyeing her from the top of the full-length mirror.

"Do you think Ears will like it?" She fingered her hair, which she had pulled back from her face with a wide barrette. The rest lay in curls on her shoulders.

"I'm absolutely sure of it."

"I wish Mother were here," Elise said, lifting the lid of the carved box. She fingered the strand of pearls, remembering the way they used to lay on her mother's skin.

"I know, kid. She would be proud of you."

"Time to leave!" Elise's dad called from downstairs. "We mustn't keep Mrs. Gillum and Garren waiting."

Elise closed the box. "I wish Ears was picking me up. I feel funny, going with Garren and his mom."

"Not to worry," Herbie said. "Ears and Dawn will be waiting for you in the foyer. Lots of middle school dates don't start until both parties arrive at the destination."

Elise swirled once more in front of the mirror, then took a long look. From her black patent leather shoes to her sparkly earrings, everything looked perfect. *I wonder what Dawn is wearing?* she thought for the thousandth time.

"It doesn't matter, kid," Herbie said, smiling. "You look great!"

"Elise!" her father called.

"On my way!" Elise grabbed her coat and turned toward the door. "Are you coming, Herbie?"

"Uh, uh. I've got some important stuff to do."

"But what if I need . . ."

Herbie waved aside the question. "You'll be just fine." He produced a roll of tiny gold floss and, fluttering an inch from the mirror, began flossing his gold teeth. "Have fun!" he called, leaning closer to check the shine on his gold incisor.

Garren's mom looked great. She wore a black dress with long, dangling gold earrings. Garren opened the door for her and they got in back.

"Thanks for the ride," Mrs. Gillum said.

"Our pleasure, I'm sure," Elise's dad said, looking in the rearview mirror.

"Hi," Garren said.

"Hi," Elise replied.

No one spoke. The only sound was the car heater, blowing hot air. Outside, the frozen snow crunched under the tires. Elise felt a little sick. She took a deep breath, willed herself not to be nervous. The silence was thick and awkward. She glanced over at her dad.

Please, God, she prayed. *Don't let this evening be a disaster!*

"Looks like we'll have a white Christmas," Garren said from the back seat, trying to make conversation.

Elise smiled back at him. He looked handsome in his black suit—and he was carrying a corsage box. Dawn should be happy.

I have created you and cared for you since you were born . . . I made you and I will care for you.
(Isaiah 46:3–4 TLB)

Chapter
21

The gym was even more beautiful than Elise had imagined. For days the student council had been working secretly behind windows covered with newspaper to transform it into a winter wonderland. Huge snowflakes with sparkly glitter hung from the ceiling. Giant, live Christmas trees lined the sides, their white lights winking through tons of tinsel. An enormous silver ball hung in the center of the room, revolving slowly and sending prisms of light dancing into every corner. A table with a red cloth held big glass bowls of punch and long trays of cookies decorated with red and green sprinkles. In one corner a disc jockey from the high school's radio station was playing records.

Elise stood next to Ears, touching the wrist corsage he had given her. White carnations with holly and a pine sprig. "Thanks again for the flowers," she said as the music died down.

"No problem-o!" he said. He wore dress pants, a tux shirt, and red suspenders. His tennis shoes tapped time as the next song started. "Does this guy know how to boom the tunes or what!"

Elise nodded. All last week she'd listened to her tapes cranked up loud, hoping to get used to the noise level. She was glad now she had.

Across the floor, Elise saw Dawn and Garren. As soon as they'd arrived, Dawn had whisked him away to "introduce" him to her friends. *Show off to her friends is more like it,* Elise thought, watching Dawn drag Garren from one cluster of people to the next. She had her arm looped through his and kept pointing to the corsage perched on her shoulder. Dawn's dress was ravishing, with sequins and a short skirt. Elise looked for Riley, although she knew she wouldn't be there. She recognized some other kids she knew, and they exchanged waves.

"Wanna dance?" Ears said.

Elise didn't want to dance, but what else were you supposed to do? They'd been hanging out at the punch bowl for almost half an hour. A peppy, off-beat song with lots of drums was playing. The kids were fast dancing, doing no step in particular, to the rhythm. She and Ears blended in.

"My moves are better when I have wheels under me," Ears said, shuffling his feet.

Elise smiled. *Say something!* But she could think of nothing to say.

"But at least if I run over you this way, it won't hurt so much." Ears whirled around behind her and she turned to face him.

"I appreciate that." The music stopped and they walked to the sidelines. Elise spotted her dad across the room, standing by one of the doors. He'd been given an assignment for the evening—to make sure kids didn't sneak out before the dance was over. He looked very serious standing there beside Entrance 6, his brown suit almost acceptable with the new tie Elise had talked him into buying. He didn't seem to notice her. He was busy watching someone across the room. It was Garren's mom. For a reason she couldn't explain, Elise felt suddenly annoyed.

The evening progressed, with glasses of punch and lots of cookies and an occasional dance. They talked to Ears's friends, many of whom were eighth graders.

"So how's seventh grade the second time around?" one of them teased.

"About half as much as fun as it was the first time," Ears answered, laughing at his own good humor. Elise admired the way he never let things get him down.

Dawn and Garren always seemed to be on the opposite side of the room from wherever Ears and Elise were. *Some double date*, she thought. *I wonder if Garren is having a good time.*

"And now, dudes and dudettes," the disc jockey said, "here's a blast from the past!"

The floor cleared, and suddenly the room rocked with the sounds of "I wanna hold your hand! I wanna hold your hand, and, and. I wanna hold your hand." The Beatles. Elise's favorite! She had her mother's entire album collection. Even *Sergeant Pepper*. Then, suddenly, Garren was standing beside her.

"I think this is our dance," he said.

She smiled and took his hand as he led her to the dance floor. They fell into an easy rhythm.

"Remember the first time I found you with your albums?" he asked over the music.

Elise nodded. "You turned the bass all the way up so

94

I could *feel* the beat, even though I couldn't hear the music."

"And we did crazy, funky moves all over your living room."

"One of the first things I did when I got home from Boston was put on those Beatles records. Then I called you . . ." Suddenly Elise saw Dawn glaring from the sidelines. Her arms were folded across her chest and she looked mad. Elise swallowed. "Umm . . . how are you and Dawn getting along?" she asked as the music stopped and they walked over to get some punch.

A small wrinkle formed in Garren's forehead. "Okay, I guess. She sort of likes to . . . have things her own way."

"There you two naughty things are!" Dawn bubbled, linking her arm through Garren's again. "I turned my back for one second, and he was gone. You fickle thing, you!" Dawn said, playfully poking Garren's cheek with her finger.

Garren sighed. "How about some punch, Dawn?"

"What a delightful idea! But first I have someone I want you to meet . . ." As she and Garren moved across the dance floor, he looked back and gave Elise a small smile.

Soon it was time for the last dance. The disc jockey put on "I'm Dreaming of a White Christmas" and the lights dimmed. Every couple jammed onto the floor. Awkwardly, Ears put his hands on Elise's waist. She rested hers on his shoulders. They swayed, not too close, as the singer crooned, "Where treetops glisten . . ." Then Elise saw them. She could hardly believe her eyes. Her father was dancing with Garren's mom! And they were gliding, ballroom style, around the floor, staring into each other's eyes. Some of the kids pointed toward them and smiled. Elise looked down. How embarrassing! They were grown-ups, for Pete's sake. Why were they acting like teenagers?

Elise said good-bye to Ears before she went to join her dad. "Thanks. I had a nice time."

"Me too. Same time next year?" Ears asked. They laughed and waved good-bye.

"Whew! I made it!" Garren said, taking Elise's elbow and steering her toward the door. "Let's get out of here before the barracuda finds one more friend to introduce me to."

Elise's dad brought the car around for the three of them, then jumped out and opened the front passenger's door. Elise stepped forward, but he said, "Why don't you and Garren sit in back this time?"

"Oh, Clarence," Garren's mom laughed, swinging her high-heeled legs into the front seat. "I feel like I've just been to the prom!"

Well you haven't! Elise fumed, slamming the back car door harder than was necessary.

☆ ☆ ☆

Even in laughter the heart may ache.
(Proverbs 14:13)

96

Chapter 22

"So, how was your Christmas vacation?" Riley banged her locker shut and spun the combination lock.

"Some parts of it were great. And some parts of it were pretty weird."

"Let's start with the weird parts."

"Well, Garren's mom had us over for Christmas dinner. She'd even bought gifts for us."

"What's so weird about that? You live next door to her, don't you?"

"Sure, but she never seemed to notice us before—except for that casserole she sent over the day we moved in."

"So why all the interest now?" Riley asked as they neared their English class.

Elise sighed. "Don't breathe a word of this, Riley. But I think she likes my dad."

Riley stopped inside the door beside Elise's desk. "What do you mean, *likes*?"

"You know . . . like in boyfriend/girlfriend. At the Christmas dance they . . . well, they danced and laughed and smiled at each other. *They're* the ones who needed a chaperon, not us kids. And ever since, it's been a little weird."

Riley let out a low whistle. "Sounds like something out of a late movie I once saw. Woman next door puts moves on single professor. Persuades him to send only daughter away to low-budget boarding school. Moves in on his Shakespeare collection." Riley shrugged. "Maybe she's only after him so he'll shovel her driveway."

"Garren already does that. I wish she'd just leave Daddy alone."

"Hey, kid!" Herbie said, appearing suddenly in front of Elise. "Your dad has a right to a life of his own. These last two years have been pretty rough on him, too."

"I don't want somebody trying to replace my mother!" Elise said.

"Whoa!" Riley said, holding her hands up in front of her. "I didn't say you did."

"Sorry," Elise said, swiping at Herbie with her hand. "I was talking to . . . myself."

"Okay," Riley continued. "What was the *great* part of your vacation?"

Elise smiled. "My Aunt Wanda showed up unexpectedly from Indianapolis and took me shopping in Chicago. We hit the after-Christmas sales at Marshall Field's and Water Tower. She has the best taste in clothes!"

Just then Dawn walked in wearing a snazzy new outfit with matching leather boots.

"Looks like Santa was good to Little Miss Rah-Rah,"

Riley said, picking up her books and heading for her seat.

"Hi, Dawn," Elise said. She hadn't talked to Dawn since the Christmas dance. "Nice outfit."

"Oh, hi!" Dawn said. "Isn't it a drag to be back in school? I'd hardly started listening to all my new CD's. And I have about a gazillion clothes to return to the mall." She flipped her hair back over her shoulder. "How's Garren?"

Elise shrugged. "Okay, I guess."

"All right, class! Let's settle down!" Miss Rosetti said, closing the door as everyone scurried to their seats. Everyone except Dawn, who walked slowly in front of the whole class to her desk on the opposite side of the room.

"I have an important announcement to make." Miss Rosetti smiled, like she was about to tell some huge, wonderful secret. "There's going to be a school-wide contest."

"What kind of contest?" one of the boys yelled out from the back.

Miss Rosetti continued. "Because Hinkle Creek is a fairly new school, it's taken a few years to generate a sense of school spirit. But now the Hinkle Creek Knights are known citywide for excellence in football, basketball, track—even wrestling."

Elise began thumbing through her literature book. A sports contest. Competitive sports didn't interest her that much, except for Garren's wrestling. What chance would she have in a sports contest?

". . . decided it's time for a school song. And instead of the faculty coming up with some old, stuffy melody, we're opening it to the entire school. We're looking for the best school song ever! You may want to try writing one yourself, or team up with some friends."

A school song? Elise thought about the pack of poems that she'd written. They were stashed in her bottom dresser drawer under her sweatshirts. Some of them were pretty good. Even Riley thought so. Coming up with some song lyrics might be fun.

"What's the prize?" Alissa asked.

Miss Rosetti's smile grew even larger. "A gift certificate to Blythe's Sporting Goods."

"How much?" one of the boys asked.

"One hundred dollars!"

Wow! A hundred dollars! The whole room buzzed as the kids whispered excitedly.

The boys began scooting their desks together, asking who'd ever had music lessons or been in choir. Elise looked across at Dawn and Alissa. They already had their heads together. Who better than cheerleaders to write a new school song? *What chance have I got?* Elise thought. *I've never even been to a football or a basketball game.*

Miss Rosetti clapped her hands. "You have six weeks to write your song. You can submit either a written version, a tape of someone singing the song, or both. The faculty will choose the best three entries, and then the whole student body will vote on which song wins. I'll be happy to answer any questions you might have after class. Now, let's tackle some grammar."

The whole student body will vote. Elise glanced over at Dawn in her perfect new outfit—and knew that *who* you were was going to be just as important as the song you wrote. *And I'm nobody, that's who I am!*

As Elise reached for her spiral, she saw Riley trying

to get her attention. A strange smile was on her face. "Wait for me after school," she mouthed. Then she gave her the "thumbs-up" sign.

Elise nodded. *What's gotten into Riley?* she wondered, pulling out her capitalization homework and wishing Miss Rosetti had never even mentioned this stupid song contest.

Whatever your hand finds to do, do it with all your might.

(*Ecclesiastes 9:10*)

Chapter

23

"We can do it, I tell you!"

"You're crazy!" Elise told Riley. She cupped her hands around her hot chocolate and looked out at the dirty snow in McDonald's parking lot. "What chance could we have against Dawn and Alissa?"

"What's so special about Dawn and Alissa?" Riley asked, saying their names in a sing-songy way.

"Well, they've been to every athletic event since they learned to walk." Elise hesitated. She didn't want to hurt Riley's feelings, but . . . "And they're popular. If the whole school is going to vote . . ."

Riley dipped her finger into the small container of honey and then carefully licked it off. Elise could almost hear her brain gears turn.

"Let's be logical about this," Riley said. "You're a good poet, right?"

Elise nodded. "Pretty good, I guess."

"And I've had music lessons since I could sit up. Piano and flute and cello. I have more melodies bopping around in my head than most radio stations have in their entire collection. With our combined talent, we should be able to write a school song in the time it takes Dawn and Alissa to blow dry their hair!"

"But the whole school is going to vote, Riley. Who would vote for us?"

Riley leaned back and slowly chewed her last french fry. "Who's the most popular person at Hinkle Creek?"

Elise sipped her hot chocolate. "Boy or girl?"

Riley smiled. "Person."

"Dawn is pretty popular. And some of the eighth grade cheerleaders. Probably the captain of the football team—"

Riley smacked her hand down on the table. "Wrong! The most popular person at Hinkle Creek is the mysterious, elusive, witty, intelligent, articulate, popular . . . *phantom!*"

Elise almost choked on her hot chocolate. It was true. After every newspaper issue, the halls buzzed for days with kids repeating the clever things The Phantom had said, with their guessing who he might be. Even Dawn had said what a shame to be popular and not take advantage of it.

"But I don't think I could do the music part . . ."

"Hey," Riley said, pointing at herself with her thumb. "You got me, babe. Miss Music herself. We'll team up, write the song, submit it with The Phantom's name on it—and wait to win our prize."

Elise had never seen Riley so excited. "Why is this so important to you? Is it the hundred-dollar gift certificate?"

"Are you kidding? Can you imagine me even entering a sporting goods store, much less spending a hundred bucks there?" Riley crumpled her french fry package. "I want to beat those cheerleaders on their own turf. And The Phantom's just the one to do it."

"But if we win—and that's still a big if—The Phantom will have to give up his secret identity." Elise's heart raced just thinking about it. This could make her popular. *Really* popular.

Riley stood to go. "By the time the contest is all wrapped up, it'll be close to the end of school anyway. Nothing good lasts forever." She tossed her trash into the barrel and then stuck out her hand to Elise. "So, are we a team?"

Elise stood and took her hand. "Sure. A team."

> *Two are better than one, because they have a good*
> *return for their work.*
> (Ecclesiastes 4:9)

Chapter 24

"The lyrics I've written don't fit any of these melodies Riley gave me!" Elise banged her hands on the piano keys and then winced at the sound.

"Hey, no one said it was going to be easy!" Herbie flew down and perched beside the sheets of handwritten music. He hummed as the pages turned themselves. "Some pretty good stuff here."

Coming from the kitchen were the murmur of voices and an occasional laugh as Elise's dad and Garren's mom made dinner. It was a pleasant sound, really. One that Elise was getting used to. Maybe Garren's mom was okay after all—or maybe Elise was just getting used to her. And it was good to hear her dad laugh.

Elise tinkered with the melody she liked best. It was simple, but haunting somehow, with lots of energy. "Oh, Herbie! I've just got to come up with the winning song!"

"I had no idea you were so interested in songs urging human competitors to . . ." Herbie flew around and read over Elise's shoulder. "Fight, fight, fight."

Elise flipped her spiral shut. "You don't understand, Herbie. This is my big chance."

"Big chance?"

"To be popular! If I can win this contest, I'll get invited to every party, never have to wonder where to sit in the cafeteria. The phone will ring all the time. And Dawn, well, maybe Dawn really *will* want to be my best friend."

"And what about Riley?" Herbie asked.

"Riley?"

"Yeah, Riley!" Herbie flew back and forth in midair, his halo hardly able to keep up with his pacing. "You remember her. Your current best friend. The one responsible for half of this creative endeavor."

"I can still be friends with Riley."

"Is that so?" Herbie grew calm and flew down to look Elise in the eye. "Listen, kid. It won't matter who else likes you if you don't like yourself."

"Don't preach at me, Herbie! I want to fit in! And this song is my ticket out of nobody's-ville."

"You know, it bothers the Boss a lot when you humans talk like that."

"Like what?" Elise said, gathering up the music.

"Saying you're nobody. *Everybody's* somebody! He wouldn't have it any other way. You are made in God's image. Even we angels can't make that boast. Lots of people love you and care what happens to you. And so does God."

Elise sighed. "I know that, Herbie. I just want to be part of the popular group. Is that so bad?"

"Everything has a price tag, kid. Just be sure you're not paying too much for this popularity stuff."

Elise fingered the keys, fiddling with the song melodies. "I'll be okay, Herbie." She smiled up at him.

"After all, I've got my very own guardian angel watching out for me for the rest of my life."

Herbie shuffled his feet nervously along the keys. "Um . . . the rest of your life is a long time, kid. And there are other people . . ."

"Hey, Herbie!" Elise said, "I know that song you're playing! Can you really play the piano?"

Herbie puffed his chest out proudly and dragged his big toe across the keyboard. "Can snowflakes fall?"

"How about a duet? What other songs do you know?" Elise asked.

"Only everything!" Herbie said, his gold teeth gleaming.

"Dinner!" Garren's mom called from the kitchen.

"In a minute!" Elise said, as a jazzy version of *Heart and Soul* echoed through the house.

"This is my favorite line," Riley said, reading Elise's lyrics for the third time. "'Always working, never shirking.' I think we're getting close, really close."

Elise hoped so. For a month now, she and Riley had been working secretly on the school song. Lots of kids had already turned in their entries. But Riley kept reminding Elise that it wasn't a race, it was a contest. "I'd rather be last and best," Riley had said. "And I'm sure The Phantom feels the same way."

Riley stuffed the latest lyrics into her notebook. "Let me take them home." She lowered her voice to a whisper. "And see how they sound with the music. I'll call you later."

Elise waved and started down the hall. She was halfway to gym class when she clasped her hand over her mouth, realizing she had been humming their secret melody.

Sing and make music in your heart to the Lord, always giving thanks to God the Father for everything, in the name of our Lord Jesus Christ.
(Ephesians 5:19)

Chapter 25

It seemed like every kid in the school was crowded around the cafeteria window where the list had been hung. Disappointed grunts and moans drifted through the crowd.

"We're not on it!" one girl shrieked.

"Drat!" a big boy said, smashing his fist into his science book when he saw his name was not among the three finalists. "There goes my new tennis shoes."

"Can you see anything?" Elise asked Riley as they worked their way toward the front of the mob. It reminded Elise of the windows at Marshall Field's when she and Aunt Wanda had gone shopping. Every window was decorated with a fantastic Christmas scene, complete with moving elves and reindeer. People lined up five and six deep, waiting for a chance to get close to the displays.

Riley shook her head. "Not yet. But the list is short enough so that even those jocks with double-digit IQ's can read it quick. Just stick with me." Riley pushed forward, pulling Elise with her.

Finally, they stood in front of the posted list. The

first paragraph thanked everyone for their entries. But the information everybody cared about was carefully typed and centered in the middle of the white page.

FINALISTS FOR SCHOOL SONG
Carol Heimberg and P.J. Henson
Jeff Larson
The Phantom

Elise gasped. They had made it! "Riley!" she began, but Riley gave her a quick look and shook her head. Of course! They had to keep quiet about their identities until The Phantom had won.

"Suppose The Phantom has a chance?" Riley asked, her tone impersonal and cool.

Elise pulled her spiral up to cover the smile that wouldn't stay down and shrugged her shoulders.

"Oh, pooh!" Elise heard Dawn moan from nearby. "We didn't make it! Probably a fixed contest," she huffed.

Alissa said, "I told you we shouldn't repeat the same words every other line."

"But I liked that line!" Dawn stood staring at the list. "Well, it's obvious who I'm voting for. If I . . . er, *we* have to lose, I'm going to make sure it's not to an ordinary person. I'm voting for The Phantom." She turned toward the dwindling crowd and, in her best cheerleading voice, yelled: "Phantom for winner! Phantom for winner!" She wove her way through the crowd, working them with her perfect smile, persuading a few to join in her chant.

Riley raised her fist into the air. "Phantom for winner! Phantom for winner!"

111

Elise let her smile burst through and joined in.

"Can you believe it, Herbie?" Elise stood at the kitchen sink, doing the dinner dishes. "We made it to the finals!"

Herbie yawned. "Of course I can believe it. I mean, I've seen the Red Sea divide and the sun stand still and the rock at Christ's tomb rolled away . . ."

Elise ran the skillet under the water and looked at Herbie. "Herbie, can you . . . you know, tell the future?"

Herbie humphed. "You humans don't need to know the future. You have enough trouble just handling the present!"

"But do you know if I'm going to win?" She put away the last pan and stood drying her hands on a dish towel.

"If *you're* going to win? I thought this was a team effort."

Elise flipped off the light and started for her room. "It was . . . I mean is. It's just that I really have been The Phantom all year."

Herbie flew up the steps behind her. "And whose idea was it to make *you* this mysterious phantom?"

Elise thought back to that day at McDonald's. "Riley's."

"And who edited your copy and helped you think of ideas?"

"Riley."

"And who suggested you enter this contest in the first place?"

"Okay, Herbie. I get it!" Elise said, kicking off her

shoes and walking to her closet. *I've got to wear something really cool tomorrow. I've got to look just perfect.*

"How you look won't influence the voters, kid. After all, they all have their own picture of who The Phantom is. And sometimes reality can be a little disappointing when you've lived with an illusion for months."

Elise turned to look at Herbie. "What do you mean by that?"

"Ah," Herbie said, wind chime laughter echoing around the room, "that comes under the heading of 'future.'" And in a flurry of angel dust, he disappeared.

I've got to win. I've just got to! Elise thought, turning back to her closet. *And when I do win, nobody's going to mess it up for me!*

But she could almost hear Riley's voice asking, "So, are we a team?"

Therefore do not worry about tomorrow, for tomorrow will worry about itself. Each day has enough trouble of its own.
(Matthew 6:34)

Chapter 26

Elise couldn't wait to get to school. The three songs were scheduled to be played over the intercom as soon as homeroom attendance had been taken.

"Who are you voting for?" It was the question everyone asked each other as they hurried down the noisy halls.

"I'm voting for The Phantom."

Elise heard the reply over and over. And every time she heard it, her heart beat a little faster. *I just might win!* she thought, hugging her books and smiling at everyone she met.

Elise passed the choir room, where the eighth grade chorus was busy warming up. Soon they would file down to the office and sing each song into the school PA system. Voting would take place during lunch.

Just before she reached homeroom, Elise saw Dawn and Alissa in front of their lockers. "Hi," she said, hoping they'd notice. But they were busy talking about the contest.

"I tell you, it's going to be The Phantom by a landslide!" Dawn said, banging her locker shut.

"But I hear Jeff's song is pretty good," Alissa said.

"This isn't just about a song!" Dawn said, her voice loud as she turned to face Alissa. "The winner has to be somebody special. And Jeff is *really* ordinary."

"But we don't even know who The Phantom is!"

Dawn's dark eyes danced with excitement. "But we will if he wins! I'm giving a huge party on Saturday night, and I plan to make The Phantom my guest of honor. Winning this contest is sure to flush him out."

"Any ideas who it might be?"

"I think it's an eighth grader," Dawn said, her voice husky with excitement. "Some big hunk of an athlete who's not afraid to say what he thinks."

"It could be a girl," Alissa reminded her.

Dawn humphed and waved the idea aside with her hand. "There's only one way to find out. Vote for The Phantom!"

Dawn and Alissa brushed past Elise on their way to homeroom. *Wait until they find out I'm The Phantom,* Elise thought as she hurried down the hall. *Then they'll notice me.* But she felt herself shiver when she remembered Herbie's words from the night before: "Sometimes reality can be a little disappointing when you've lived with an illusion for months."

The other two songs were first. Elise listened along with the rest of the school. They were good. Maybe too good to beat. Then the principal announced the last song, The Phantom's song. As soon as he said the word *Phantom,* the class burst into applause. They were hardly quiet by the time the song started. Elise listened to the words and melody, humming along in her head.

The Knights will fight for right and honor
The Knights will fight through thick and thin
The Knights will fight; no foe's too mighty
The Knights will fight until they win!

The kids were tapping their feet. A few bobbed their heads to the pulsing rhythm as the chorus launched into the second verse. Then it was over. The principal thanked everyone for their attention and participation before clicking off the sound system.

Now all Elise could do was wait until lunch.

At the end of the cafeteria was a table with a big black box. The student council president handed out ballots to the long line of kids waiting to vote. One by one the pieces of paper were folded and dropped into the box. Elise got in line to vote. Riley came up behind her.

"Where you been?" Riley asked as she dug a pencil out of her back pocket. "I haven't seen you all day."

Elise shrugged. "Around."

"So," Riley said, raising her voice, "what do you think our chances are?"

Elise looked at her in horror. "Shhhh!" she said, putting her finger to her lips.

Riley laughed. Several kids in line turned around. For a split second Elise thought Riley was going to blow the whole thing. It would be just like her, too. To throw away this chance to be popular with the entire school.

"I'm voting for The Phantom," Elise said, her voice icy and firm. "How about you?"

Riley shrugged. "I haven't decided yet."

School was almost over when the crackling sound

from the PA interrupted Miss Rosetti's class. "Ladies and gentlemen," the principal began. "We have a winner!"

Elise tried to swallow the panic she felt rising in her throat. *What if I don't win?* She glanced at Riley, who had her nose stuck in an opened paperback book.

"The winner is—The Phantom, for his song 'Knights Fight!'"

Elise clapped along with everyone. *His* song. Soon everybody would know whose song it really was!

When the dismissal bell rang, Elise bolted from the room without waiting for Riley.

> *Beware! Don't always be wishing for what you don't have.*
>   Luke 12:15 (TLB)

Chapter

27

"I won! I won! I won!" Elise whispered the words to herself, turned them into a chant as she rushed down the icy sidewalk toward home. *Now what? How can I let everybody know The Phantom is really me? What I need is a plan . . .*

"Yo! Obviously a contestant for the 'World Power Walk' championships."

Elise turned to see Ears hurrying to catch up with her. Fat red earmuffs covered the earphones plugged into his head. As he came up beside her, he clicked off his tape.

"Off to a two-for-one sale somewhere I don't know about?" he asked, his breath making a tiny cloud in front of his mouth.

Elise shook her head. "Just want to get home."

"Doesn't everybody!" Ears said, falling in step with Elise's brisk walk. "If only home didn't mean *homework.* Mr. Hoffer gets meaner by the year. And I'm the guy who knows."

Elise nodded. She didn't want to talk now. She had important things to think about.

"So, what do you think about the school song? Like, do you like the winner?" Ears asked.

"You mean The Phantom?"

Ears laughed into the icy air. "No, I mean the song. After all, it was a *song* contest."

"Sure, I like it. A lot." She waited for Ears to speculate who The Phantom might be. He didn't. "Do you like it?"

"It's okay. I thought the line about 'always working, never shirking' was a little much."

Elise walked even faster. What did Ears know about music? Poetry? Anything!

"I was wondering," Ears said, almost running now to keep up with her, "if you'd like to see a flick Saturday night. My youth group at church is having 'Cinema Night' with popcorn and sodas and about a million movies."

A date! He's asking me for another date! Elise felt her heartbeat speed up even though she slowed her steps. "Thanks. I'd love to . . ."

Dawn's party! The Phantom's big moment. It was supposed to be Saturday night—wasn't that what Dawn had said?

". . . but I can't. I have to . . . to . . ."

"Hey, I understand. Sometimes a person just has to . . . to." Without another word, Ears clicked on his tape player and turned down the street that led to his part of town.

Elise watched him go, listening to the crunch of his hightop sneakers in the cold snow. It was good to hear. Sometimes she forgot to remember just how good. *I hope I didn't make him mad. But I can't think about that.* She bent into the wind and picked up her pace again. *Now, about my plan . . .*

When Elise got to her front steps, she could hear the phone ringing. Fumbling with the key, she finally unlocked and pushed open the heavy oak door.

"Hello?" she yelled into the receiver, her chest heaving with the hurry of getting inside.

"Elise? Uh . . . it's me. You know, Riley."

It didn't sound like Riley. Riley was always so sure of herself, her words spitting out like well-aimed watermelon seeds. "Hi." Elise fingered the phone cord. She didn't want to talk to Riley. Not now.

"Well, we did it. Huh?"

We. Elise had stopped thinking with the plural days ago. *I did it*, she thought. But she mumbled a "Guess so."

"And now The Phantom has to write his 'coming-out-of-the-closet' column. I've been thinking about what we could say."

There it was. That *we* again. When had Riley ever written a Phantom column?

Riley went on, her voice tight and quick. "Why don't we do a satire about contests? How many people get ripped off each year in them? Interview a few people who lost in that stupid school song contest."

"I don't think it was a stupid contest." Elise said it slowly, with a space between each word.

Silence. "Okay, forget the stupid part," Riley said. Elise could almost see her twirling her hair, the way she did sometimes when she was trying to come up with ideas for the newspaper. "How about we issue a plea to the administration to take that hundred dollar cer-

120

tificate, convert it into cash, and use it to better the school. Fund a few new projects."

"Like what?" Elise asked. *That's my hundred dollars we're talking about!*

Riley was more herself now, the ideas coming one after the other. "How about buying giant note pads to hang in the johns so the kids won't have to write on the walls? Or new ties for the faculty. I know! They could put Pepto-Bismol bottles next to the catsup on every table in the cafeteria!" Riley laughed, but the silence from Elise's end seemed to drown out the sound.

"I have to go, Riley," Elise said. "My . . . my dad will be home any minute and I have to start dinner."

"Sure. I'll see you tomorrow." *Click.*

Not if I see you first. It had been a joke between Elise and her mom. If one of them said, "See you later" the other would always reply, "Not if I see you first!" But as Elise set the phone down, she knew this was no joke. She didn't want to see Riley. At least not until she'd come up with a plan.

For there is a proper time and procedure for every matter.

(Ecclesiastes 8:6)

Chapter

28

It had been almost midnight when the plan had come to her.

Elise stood in the school hallway, checking her folder every few minutes to make sure she had everything she needed. She pressed her forehead against the door glass and looked outside. Where was Dawn? There! Elise spotted her leather coat. She was carrying her cheerleading pompons and giggling with the group of girls that surrounded her. Elise swallowed and willed her knees not to shake. It was a good plan. It would work. It *had* to work. Otherwise Riley might mess up everything.

"Dawn!" Elise shouted loudly as Dawn pushed open the door and stomped her snow-covered boots on the rubber mat. Dawn glanced toward her. Without waiting for a response, Elise came up next to her. "Hi! Boy, isn't it cold today?"

"It usually is in February." Dawn scanned the halls for some of her friends.

Don't let her get away! As Dawn started for her locker, Elise walked with her. "So, The Phantom won!"

"Thanks in no small part to me," Dawn said, brushing snow off her mittens. "He owes me big time, and the sooner he finds it out the better."

Elise felt uncomfortable. Would Dawn be disappointed when she found out The Phantom was a girl? That The Phantom was an *ordinary* girl like her? "Dawn," Elise began, "suppose The Phantom turns out to be a girl."

"Fat chance," Dawn said. But suddenly she stopped and turned around. "Do you know who The Phantom is?" Her eyes gleamed as she pushed Elise to the side of the hall. "You know, don't you!"

"Well, I *am* on the newspaper staff . . ."

"That's right! Oh, tell! You must tell! It's an eighth grader, isn't it?"

Elise shook her head. "Seventh." Dawn looked disappointed. "But The Phantom is older than most other kids in seventh grade." She was enjoying Dawn's attention, wishing this moment could last all day.

"What team is he on? Football? Wrestling? Basketball?"

Elise felt a lump form in her throat. "Well, he's not exactly on a team."

"Not on a team? Of course he's on a team! He wrote the school song, didn't he? Some nerdy egghead couldn't write a school song like that, full of might and fight."

This is harder than I thought. The first bell rang. "It's me," Elise blurted out.

"It's you what?"

"I'm The Phantom."

Dawn looked at her closely. "I don't think it's very

nice of you to joke about something as sacred as our school song . . ."

Elise opened her folder and pulled out the original copy of the school song. It was written in her own handwriting. And last night, under the words "by The Phantom" Elise had inked in her own name. Dawn held the evidence, her mouth open in surprise. Two tiny wrinkles creased the center of her forehead. "You're . . . you're The Phantom?"

"At your service." Elise half bowed, but Dawn didn't seem amused.

"You wrote all that Phantom stuff? And the school song?"

"Yes, I did." Elise pulled the other Phantom newspaper columns out of her folder. "See. Mine. All mine."

Dawn was disappointed. Elise could see that. But soon a mischievous smile replaced her frown. "Does anyone else know?"

"Nobody." *Riley knows, but to Dawn Riley has always been nobody anyway.*

Just then Alissa came up. "Hi, Dawn. Can I copy your math homework?"

Dawn grabbed Alissa's arm and pulled her close. "I know who The Phantom is!" she squealed.

"Who?"

Dawn smiled, obviously proud of her confidential information. "It's a secret. Isn't that right, Elise?"

"Sure," Elise said, trying to follow what was happening. "A secret."

"But I'm your best friend!" Alissa whined. "Can't you tell me?"

"Well, I guess best friends can share secrets. But mum's the word!" Dawn looped one arm through

Dawn's and one through Elise's as they walked down the hall, their heads bent close together.

* * *

Elise was hungry. Even the school's spaghetti looked good to her. She held her tray, scanning the tables for a place to sit. So far, so good. She hadn't seen Riley once.

"Hey, Elise."

The voice came from so close by that it made Elise jump. There sat Riley, with an empty place next to her. "Take a load off."

Just then, Dawn stood up and yelled across the cafeteria. "Oh, Elise! Over here! Do come eat with us!"

Elise felt her appetite drain away. She glanced down at Riley. "Thanks, but I . . . I think I'll eat over there . . . for today."

Riley's eyes were cold. She jabbed her fork into the mountain of spaghetti and spun it around. "No problem, Elise. Or should I call you Phantom?"

Several kids looked up, but Elise hurried toward Dawn's table. She'd promised Dawn she wouldn't tell anyone. That Dawn herself could announce who The Phantom was at her party Saturday night.

"Not a good move, kid," Herbie said, balancing himself on the edge of Elise's tray.

"Look, Herbie. It's a free country. I can eat lunch anywhere I want to."

"I wasn't just referring to your choice of seating."

"Not now," Elise said through clenched teeth as she neared the table. "I've got to talk to my friends."

"In case you've forgotten, kid, *I'm* your friend! So is

Riley. And if you're looking to expand your circle of friends, why not sit with Melinda?"

Elise saw Melinda sitting alone at the end of the last table. She remembered how Dawn had made fun of Melinda last fall when the first Phantom column came out. How she'd called her a pig in front of everyone.

"Here, here, here!" Dawn said, patting a place the girls had cleared beside her.

Elise turned her back on Melinda and sat down.

> *. . . have a clean conscience and desire to live honorably in every way.*
> (*Hebrews 13:18*)

Chapter 29

Dawn's basement room was full of kids—wall-to-wall movement and noise. In one corner a loud stereo boomed out rock music. Elise sat on the edge of her chair, looking for someone she knew. Most of the kids were older. Eighth graders, maybe. But some looked old enough to be in high school. A few acknowledged her with a nod. One girl from her gym class waved from across the room. Dawn was nowhere in sight.

"Hey, cutie. How about a dance?" A big boy with dark eyes stood in front of Elise. An earring dangled from one ear, and his hair was long and tangled.

"No," Elise said, louder than she'd intended to.

He took a step back and snorted. "I ain't deaf, man!"

No, but I used to be, Elise thought. *What would this guy think if I told him that? What would they all think?*

"Is everybody hungry?" Dawn came down the steps, carrying pizzas. "Come and get it!" She hardly made it to the table before hands were grabbing for pieces. "Naughty, naughty!" she said, slapping the hands of a cute guy wearing a high school letter jacket. "You have to learn to ask for what you want."

Elise sipped her glass of cola, waiting for the pizza crowd to thin out. So far, the party hadn't been much fun. *Maybe you're the one who's not much fun*, she told herself, watching several boys shake up cans of pop and then open them, spraying each other and anyone else who happened to get too close.

Elise chose the first piece of pizza she could reach. Not until she was seated on a folding chair in the corner did she realize it had mushrooms on it. *Yuck!* One by one she picked them off and laid them on her plate.

"What you need is something to wash those down with." It was the boy again. He was sort of smiling and holding out a can to her.

"I already had something to drink, thank you." Elise pretended to be very interested in her pizza.

"Not like this, baby!" He popped open the can and pushed it towards her. Beer. It was beer!

"I . . . I don't like it."

"I bet you never even tried it." He pulled a chair close to hers. "Just a little sip." Elise could smell the beer on his breath. "It's good stuff, you'll see."

Elise wanted to run. Or scream.

"Now, Darrien, are you bothering my friend here?" Dawn put her hand on Darrien's shoulder.

"Naw! I'm just trying to introduce her to some of the finer things in life."

"Listen, why don't you go sit with Alissa? She's been asking about you."

Instantly Darrien was gone. Elise tried to pick up her pizza, but her hands were shaking. "Thanks, Dawn," she said.

Dawn laughed. "He's harmless, actually. Just likes to tease shy girls."

128

"When are we going to . . . you know, make the announcement?" Elise knew things would be different after they all knew she was The Phantom. Then she'd be one of them. Popular. Yes, things would be better once they knew.

"Soon. I just want to tease them a little more," Dawn said, looking around at the crowd. "Everybody is trying to figure out who The Phantom is. Let's just enjoy the suspense."

But Elise wasn't enjoying the suspense. Or much of anything else.

When the last piece of pizza was gone, devoured by a boy who folded it and slid it down his throat whole, like a fishing worm, Dawn stood up. *This is it*, Elise thought. She ran her napkin across her teeth to make sure they were clean. She smoothed her hair and sat up straight.

"Tonight is a special night," Dawn began, her smile beaming like a hundred-watt bulb. "The Phantom is in our midst!"

"Bring him on!"

"Phantom for president!"

The group was rowdy, loud. But Dawn seemed perfectly at ease. "Before our secret guest goes public, how about a game of 'Name the Nerd'?"

Name the Nerd? Elise had never heard of that game. It sounded like something Dawn would like to play, though.

Soon everyone was in a large circle. They all seemed to know how to play. Elise moved closer to watch. Maybe it would be fun.

It wasn't.

"Okay, who's this?" one boy asked, pulling off a

girl's glasses and putting them on his face. He stuck out his top teeth and pretended to be picking his nose.

"L. B. Lawrence!" Alissa squealed.

"Right! Your turn!"

L. B. Lawrence. Elise had heard about him. One of the smartest boys in school. Too smart to be popular, obviously.

Alissa was next. She puffed out her cheeks, pretended to have a huge belly, and waddled around in a circle.

"Too easy," Dawn giggled. "Melinda."

Several boys made oinking sounds. Everyone laughed. Elise was beginning to feel sick. Maybe it was the pizza.

Dawn was in the center now. She puckered up her mouth and squinted her eyes, pretending to read a book. "I just love the classics," she drawled, "and wearing the same pair of jeans every day. No one's ever seen my legs because . . . newspaper editors don't have legs!"

Riley! They were making fun of Riley!

"That newspaper chick. What's-her-name."

"Yeah," another girl said. "The one with the weird name."

"Riley," Elise said. "Her name is Riley." *And she's my friend*, Elise wanted to add. But she knew she couldn't.

"Your turn!" Dawn said, but she could tell Elise was upset and not about to take center stage. Unless . . .

"Ladies and gentlemen, the moment has arrived," Dawn said, pulling a chair to the center and standing on it. "The voice of protest and reason, the champion of every kid at Hinkle Creek. And now, the author of our new school song. May I present—The Phantom!"

Everyone waited. Several of the guys had their arms draped around girls' necks. In the back a couple was sharing a cigarette. Elise tried to step forward, but her knees seemed made of Jell-O.

Dawn seemed a bit panicked. "Now, Phantom!" She scanned the crowd until she found Elise. Their eyes met, and Elise could sense Dawn's fear. "Phantom, it's time people knew who you really are!"

"I'll drink to that," the dark-eyed boy said as he and Alissa bumped their beer cans together and laughed.

It's time people knew who you really are! Suddenly Elise found her legs. But they were carrying her up the stairs, not to the center of the room. She grabbed her coat off the couch and ran out into the frosty darkness.

Not until she was halfway home did she realize she was crying.

> *No temptation has seized you except what is common to man. And God is faithful; he will not let you be tempted beyond what you can bear. But when you are tempted, he will also provide a way out so that you can stand up under it.*
> (1 Corinthians 10:13)

132

Chapter
30

Elise woke to the sound of cold rain pounding on her window. Monday. School. She pulled the covers over her head and wished for the thousandth time that she never had to go back to Hinkle Creek again. That she never had to face Dawn and Alissa and Riley. Especially Riley.

Yesterday had been terrible. After church, she'd spent the whole day alone in her room, going over everything that had happened at Dawn's party. Trying to sort out her feelings. Haunted by all the mistakes she'd made. Missing her mother. Over and over, like a stuck record, Dawn's words had replayed in her head: "It's time people knew who you really are." *Who am I?* Elise knew it was a question she had to answer for herself.

It had been a long, lonely, difficult day. Not even Herbie had been around for company.

Herbie's probably mad at me, too. Everybody else is. Elise pushed back the covers and stared at the drops running down her window pane. As bad as yesterday had been, she was afraid today was going to be worse.

"Rise and shine, kid," Herbie said, suddenly appearing on the window ledge.

"Where have you been?" Elise asked.

Herbie laughed, and the sound of wind chimes tinkled around the room. "Here and there."

"Well," Elise said gruffly, "it must have been mostly there. I sure didn't see you around here yesterday."

"Ah," Herbie said, a gold magician's wand suddenly appearing in his hand, "what is unseen is often more real than what is seen." With a wave of the wand, he produced a bouquet of paper daisies.

Elise reached for the flowers, but they vanished before she could touch them. "Not funny, Herbie." She jammed her feet into her slippers and headed for the bathroom.

"My, my. Aren't we touchy this morning!" Herbie flew along beside her.

"And why shouldn't I be? The world's worst weekend is about to be followed by the world's worst Monday."

"So, have you taken up prophecy? Can you foretell the future?"

Elise stopped and looked at Herbie. "No, but if you'd be a little more help, maybe I wouldn't keep making a mess of everything. Some guardian angel you've turned out to be!"

"Sure, sure," Herbie said. "Blame me. Let's see . . . was I the one who suggested you take all the credit for the school song? Did I tell you to snub Riley and sit with Dawn in the cafeteria? Did I . . ."

Elise sighed. "No, Herbie. It was me. All me." Elise felt the tightness in her chest, the terror at having to face everyone. "What do I do now?"

134

"Wash your face and brush your teeth, for starters," Herbie said. "And then eat a good breakfast. It's going to be an interesting day . . ."

Elise spent the morning hurrying from class to class, looking down as much as possible. She overhead a few people mention The Phantom and the new school song. But mostly it was a new week and people were ready for something new to happen. Once Elise ducked into the girls' bathroom when she saw Dawn coming. And she had to stay bent over the drinking fountain for what seemed like forever while Riley walked past. Since she wasn't about to risk facing the cafeteria cliques, Elise spent lunch in the library, sitting on the floor between the stacks of biographies. Then, just when she thought she was going to make it through the day without a major catastrophe, came gym class.

They played volleyball, and Elise's team won. Dawn was on the losing team, but she didn't speak to Elise. Didn't even looked at her. *I'm invisible again*, Elise thought, sending the volleyball flying across the net.

The locker room was almost empty. Elise was putting on her shoes when she heard the conversation coming from the other side of the lockers.

"A total zero. I should have known better than to invite her."

It was Dawn's voice.

"Why did you?" a girl's voice asked.

"Elise told me she was going to bring The Phantom to the party."

They're talking about me! Elise held perfectly still and listened.

"And I, of course, believed her," Dawn continued.

"Stupid me! She came alone—and made a perfect fool of herself."

So, Dawn didn't tell anyone that I was The Phantom!

"She never attends any of the ball games. All Elise does is write for that dreary school newspaper. Did you know I had to arrange her date for the Christmas dance? I even doubled with one of her friends so the poor thing could go."

Elise felt anger rising in her, hot and consuming. *You used my friendship with Garren to help you get a date for the Christmas dance!*

The voices were moving away.

"I'm giving up on her. Throwing her back to the other losers she hangs around with." Dawn laughed as the door closed behind her.

"You're the loser!" Elise yelled into the empty locker room.

The drip of the showers was the only response.

☆ ☆ ☆

All the days ordained for me were written in your book before one of them came to be. How precious to me are your thoughts, O God! How vast is the sum of them!

(Psalm 139:16–17)

Chapter 31

Elise didn't go to her last period English class. She knew she couldn't face Dawn, sitting there across the room, whispering to Alissa and writing notes. Instead, she waited in the locker room until she was sure the halls would be empty. Then she walked to her locker, got her coat, and left school.

The rain had stopped, and a spring-like breeze was blowing the empty branches of the trees. The whole world seemed clean and fresh, ready for a new season to begin.

I'm ready for a change, too, Elise thought. She hurried away from school, but didn't want to go home just yet. The park! It was sure to be empty.

Elise dried off the swing seat with some napkins she found in her pocket and sat down. She grabbed the cold chains and began to pump. Higher and higher, the wind whizzing past her ears, her heart thudding in rhythm with each *swoosh*. She knew she'd made a mess of things, and now she had to put them right. But how?

"Well, you can start by forgiving yourself," Herbie said, jogging back and forth through the air to keep up with her, his wings and feet moving furiously.

"Herbie," she laughed, "you look so silly!" She slowed her swing, dragging her feet in the sand.

Herbie landed on the next swing, panting. "Whew . . . it's not easy to . . . flutter in place . . . and talk at the same time." He took a tiny gold bandanna from his sleeve and wiped sweat off his forehead.

"Oh, Herbie," Elise sighed, digging her heels deeper into the wet sand, "what am I going to do? I wish I'd never written that school song . . ." Elise stopped and smiled. "I mean, I wish *we'd* never written that song."

"Good! You're making progress already," Herbie said. "I, for one, am glad you and Riley wrote it. It's a great song! Kids and alumni will be singing it for years and years. You should be proud! I might even teach it to heaven's choir when I get back."

"I should never have told Dawn I wrote it. And I should never, never have gone to her party."

Herbie fluttered up to look Elise in the eye. "Listen, kid. You humans make mistakes. It's been going on for years. The Boss knows it's bound to happen; that's why he has such an extensive forgiveness plan."

"Forgiveness plan?"

"Sure!" Herbie continued. "All you have to do is ask and—bingo!—he'll forgive you and give you a fresh start. Of course, you have to be really sorry and very sincere . . ."

"Boy, am I sorry!" Elise said, getting up and walking toward the drinking fountain. "The only good thing about any of this is that I finally know who I am. And I'm not one of Dawn's groupies. I don't even want to be anymore."

Herbie flew with her. "I know."

Elise took a long drink and then turned to Herbie.

138

"Will you help me, really help me? If I ever needed a guardian angel, it's now."

"Sure!" Herbie said, sticking out his chest and flexing his muscles. "I'll help you."

"No more disappearing acts?"

"Well . . . uh . . . you know, us guardian angels have lots of places we have to be," Herbie squirmed. "Listen, kid," he said, his chest deflating to normal size. "The truth is, your biggest help isn't me, wonderful though I am. Your biggest help is him." Herbie pointed toward the sky, where the sun was beginning to break through. "He's *always* on your side. And with his Spirit living in you, you can do anything. Divide seas, move mountains, survive middle school. In fact, I've seen it done."

Elise smiled. "The only mountain I want to move is the one I've put between me and Riley. Any suggestions?"

Herbie pulled his sleeve in front of his face and wiggled his eyebrows. "Sounds like a job for—The Phantom!"

"What do you mean?"

"Come on, let's go home. I'll show you."

And as Elise turned toward home, Herbie riding on her shoulder, a rainbow suddenly appeared—its colorful arch filling up the whole sky.

My help comes from the Lord, the Maker of heaven and earth.

(Psalm 121:2)

Chapter

32

"Here's my column for the newspaper." Elise held the pages out to Riley. All around them computer keys clacked as the staff finished this issue of *The Crusader*. At a high table along the side, two boys worked on art for the cover.

Riley looked at Elise, a glare so cold it made Elise shiver. "I didn't know if you'd still do a column, now that you're so busy with your new friends."

"This is The Phantom's final one. And, as a matter of fact, it's about friendship, among other things."

Riley grabbed the papers from Elise's hand. "I can't wait to read it."

"And I can't wait for you to."

"Hey, Riley, can you give us a hand over here?" one of the boys called.

"Coming!"

"Riley," Elise said, reaching out to touch her arm as she turned to go, "I'm sorry. About a bunch of things. Maybe we can talk sometime soon?"

The look was as cold as ever. "Maybe."

It was on the front page when the paper came out two days later.

PHANTOM TAKES FINAL BOW

The world is full of intelligent people giving worthwhile advice. Most of us, of course, don't listen. Maybe that's why I've enjoyed writing this column so much. Some people actually did listen.

I've poked fun at everything from cafeteria food to the school administration. But there's one thing no one should ever make fun of. Friendship. Nothing is as hard to find as a true-blue, forever friend. One who accepts you for who you are, faults and all. One who forgives you when you've made a real jerk out of yourself. Everybody wants to be better—to run faster or make better grades or get rid of his zits. But in the process, don't ever lose sight of who your real friends are. I did, once. And it's a pretty lousy thing to do.

Thanks for voting for my song. It was fun writing it—with the help of my best friend. I had planned on taking off my mask and letting you all see who I really am. But a wise man (creature, really) once told me, "Reality can be a little disappointing when you've lived with an illusion." And I'd hate to disappoint all of you, my friends.

So I'll just duck behind the curtain for now. Think of me as the best part in all of you. The part that's not afraid to care about each other, to speak out about what's wrong.

And remember—The Phantom is watching!

P.S. I heard that the reason Mr. Hoffer is so mean is because his feet always hurt. So I'm giving him my $100 gift certificate, in the hopes that a new pair of tennies will improve his disposition.

Riley came up behind Elise as she was reading. "Looks pretty good, don't you think?"

Elise folded her paper. "Looks great." The two girls stood facing each other, both avoiding looking the other in the eye. "How about we stop by McDonald's for a chocolate shake after school?" Elise asked. "My treat."

Riley looked up, a slow smile forming on her face. "And some french fries with honey?"

"Sure, why not?" Elise said, smiling.

"Yeah," Riley added as together they walked toward English class. "Why not, indeed!"

Be kind and compassionate to one another, forgiving each other, just as in Christ God forgave you.
(Ephesians 4:32)

Chapter 33

Cold smoke swirled around her as Elise strained to see through its thickness. The figure. It was motioning her to come forward. Elise started toward it, but for every step she took, the figure seemed farther away. "No!" Elise screamed. "Wait for me!"

The figure turned and, miraculously, waited. Elise got closer and closer, the smoke disappearing. The figure reached out its hand. Elise strained forward, grabbing, stretching. There! The hand was warm, familiar.

And suddenly, they were in a wide open field. Mother! It was Mother! She laughed, taking Elise's other hand as they went round and round in the meadow. Daisies were everywhere, their white faces and sunny smiles bending in the breeze. A huge butterfly fluttered into sight. No, not a butterfly. An angel. Herbie! He flitted in between and around the happy pair. Finally, Elise's mother pulled her close. Elise could smell her musky perfume, feel the warmth of her body. Elise hugged her, hard. Then she turned to Herbie, her arms open wide. "How do you hug an angel?" she asked her mother.

"Very carefully!" was her reply. "Very carefully!" Herbie's wind chime laughter joined with their own and echoed over the field of daisies.

Elise woke to dawn's first sunlight streaming through her window. The dream. Finally it had an ending. Finally the fog was gone. "Herbie! Herbie!" Elise said. "Wait till you hear about my dream . . ."

The room was quiet. Too quiet. Suddenly Elise knew—Herbie was gone. "Herbie?" she asked again, softer this time. And then she saw it, lying on her pillow. A daisy. One perfect white daisy. She pressed it to her cheek, remembering again the feel of her mother's arms.

"Thanks, Herbie," Elise said. "For everything."

And from somewhere far, far away came the familiar sound of tinkling wind chimes.

☆ ☆ ☆

I am with you and will watch over you wherever you go . . . I will not leave you.
(Genesis 28:15)